HUNTED ALONG
THE RHINE

•

PETER REESE DOYLE

7733
JF
DOY

PUBLISHING

Colorado Springs, Colorado

HUNTED ALONG THE RHINE

Copyright © 1994 by Peter Reese Doyle. All rights reserved.

International copyright secured.

Library of Congress Cataloging-in-Publication Data
Doyle, Peter Reese, 1930-

    HUNTED ALONG THE RHINE / Peter Reese Doyle.

    p. cm—(Daring Family adventures ; bk 6)

    Summary: When the Daring family.goes to Germany, they are followed by remnants of the former East German Sectet Police, and everything climaxes during a chase on the Rhine River

    ISBN 1-56179-260-8

    [1. Adventure and adventurers—Fiction. 2.Germany—Fiction.

    3. Christian life—Fiction] I. Title. II. Series: Doyle, Peter

    Reese, 1930-   Daring Family adventures : bk. 6.

    PZ7.D777 Hun 1994

    [Fic]—dc20

Published by Focus on the Family Publishing, Colorado Springs, Colorado 80995.

Distributed by Word Books, Dallas, Texas.

Editor: Etta Wilson
Designer: James A. Lebbad
Cover Illlustration: Ken Spengler

Printed in the United States of America
94 95 96 97 98 99 / 10 9 8 7 6 5 4 3 2 1

For

C. Wayne Alderman

A discipler of men.

CONTENTS

CHAPTER 1

THE CROSSBOWMAN

The man crouched on the roof was almost invisible in the moonless night. He was clad in a black jacket, black trousers, and black rubber-soled shoes. A black mask covered his head and face.

He was a banker, a highly respected loan officer in one of the larger banks in Düsseldorf, Germany. His name was Fritz Heller, but none of his customers would have recognized him this night. They would have been surprised to see their respected dignified banker dressed in such clothes, crouched on a roof in the black of night. They would also have been shocked to know that he was a deadly, skilled Crossbowman. He peered through the blackness of the night, waiting for the signal.

What his customers did not know was that Fritz Heller was also a secret agent of the former East German secret police, the dreaded STASI. This puppet organization of the Soviet KGB had supposedly been disbanded since the unification of the two

Germanys—that was what the media in Europe and the Americas wanted people to believe. In fact, the organization was very much alive, although some of its people were in hiding and many of its operations had been suspended.

The remnants of the STASI were in desperate need of funds to finance their organization's espionage operations and continued efforts to disrupt the newly united Germany. Fritz Heller, crouched on the roof of a house across from the government records building, meant to help them get some money.

He asked himself how the time could pass so slowly. Again he checked the luminous dial of his watch: two minutes to go. He sighed. Glancing below, to left and right, he was reassured by the emptiness of the street. This isolated area was a strange place for a security-conscious government to keep a building for its records, but he was thankful that the streets and sidewalks were deserted. Hardly anyone came this way at this time of the night.

That was why Fritz Heller was here. And why his accomplice, who worked in the building, had assured him that the plan would work.

Suddenly a light flashed from the window across the street: once, twice, and once again.

Picking up his own flashlight, Fritz Heller waited, eyes fixed on the window from which the light had come.

The signal was repeated. This time, Heller replied:

two quick flashes, a longer one, then three more quick ones.

Jamming the flashlight into his coat pocket, he picked up the crossbow, aimed carefully through the infrared sights and squeezed the trigger.

The arrow flashed across the street and slammed into the wall of the building, beside the window from which the signal had come. The spool on the bow hummed as the fine wire attached to the arrow unwound. Then the humming stopped.

Quickly Heller put the crossbow down, picked up the pliers, and clipped the wire. Deftly he attached its end to the thicker line coiled at his feet. Then he pulled on the wire strung across the street until it was taut.

There was an answering tug from the man at the window, and the accomplice began to reel in the line. The three thin cylinders of plastic explosive tied to the thicker wire moved from one building to another as the wire was hauled in. Because of the blackness of the night, no one from the street below could have seen the wire with the moving cylinders.

The line stopped moving. Again the narrow beam of light flashed from the window across the street. At once Fritz Heller began to reel in the now-loosened line, rolling it around a large spool as it came. When he felt the end of the wire, he stuffed the spool into his pocket, picked up his crossbow, and moved carefully to the dormer window through which he'd reached the roof. Climbing back through, he entered the pitch-black room and closed the window. He drew the curtains behind him.

He took apart the crossbow in the dark, and packed it into the leather case lying beside the window. Checking to make sure that the hall light was still off, he opened the door, turned on his penlight, stepped quietly into the hall, and headed for the stairs.

When he reached the street, he moved quickly from the door of the house to a waiting van, carrying the black leather bag that contained the dismantled crossbow. The driver already had the engine running; the Crossbowman stepped into the passenger seat and the van drove quietly away.

In the building to which the bowman had delivered the explosives, another man had been very busy. Buried deep in the cellar of the building, behind thick security doors, the sound of the professionally blown safe alarmed no one.

The folders were taken swiftly out of the damaged safe. Making no effort to disguise the wreckage, the thief took a can from his case and sprayed a thick swastika on the floor. Then he left, carrying the stolen folders in his briefcase. The small door at the back of the building opened with the turn of his key. Passing through, he stepped into the street and walked away into the night.

Hours later, in mid-morning, David Curtis led Mark and Penny Daring out of the airport terminal. They were stiff from sitting in the plane that had just brought them from Athens, and grateful for the opportunity to walk and stretch.

"Boy, it's great to breathe fresh air again!" Mark exclaimed as David hailed a taxi.

"It sure is!" David agreed.

They piled into the cab and set their packs and hand luggage on the floor. David directed the driver to the address where they would be staying for the next four days. David's German was fluent; his family had lived in Germany for several years when he was young, and had insisted he continue learning the language when they'd returned to the States. Now David was glad that they had.

Penny and her brother, Mark, were fluent in French, but they knew no German. They were depending on David to steer them around for the next several days while they were in Düsseldorf, just as they had done for him in France a couple of weeks ago.

"We're staying in a house that's right on the Rhine River," David said. "The whole neighborhood was built entirely with German materials, at Hitler's orders, to prove that Germany could be independent of foreign trade. In fact, Hitler himself came to open the area when it was finished. They named the streets after top Nazi leaders. After the war, though, the city officials changed the street names to those of German heroes who'd given their lives in the attempt to get rid of Hitler."

The three of them loved history. They read all the time, and each enjoyed hearing what the others had learned.

"Gosh, it's cool in Europe in the summer!" Penny observed. She was wearing a khaki skirt and dark blouse. "Just a minute in that wind outside the station, and I was getting cold. How do the Germans stand it?"

"You've been in Africa too long, Penny!" David laughed. "Your blood's gotten thin from all that heat!"

"Well, I'm not used to being cold in July, that's for sure!" she said.

Mark agreed with his sister. "It's a good thing Dad insisted we bring our sweaters with us, or we'd freeze in two days of this!"

Mark and Penny's father, Jim Daring, was a mining engineer, and the family lived in East Africa. David's family lived in the United States, but were great friends with the Darings, and had gladly let David accept Mark's invitation to visit him for the summer.

After just a week in Africa, however, David had accompanied Mark and Penny on a trip to Egypt. They'd gone with a friend of Mr. Daring's, to help him on a project the two men had developed. From there, the project had led them to Paris, where Mark and Penny's parents had joined them. The three teenagers had had a series of adventures at each of these places, before going to the south of France and then to Greece.

"You know," David reflected, "I came to Africa five weeks ago. My folks thought I'd have a relaxing and interesting vacation. Well, it's been interesting all right, but certainly not relaxing! We've been running for our lives half the time!"

He sounded like he was complaining. Actually, scary as their adventures had been, he wouldn't have missed them.

"Well," Mark said with a straight face, "you live in the fast lane all right! Gosh, before you came, Penny and I had a wonderful peaceful life. At this rate, we won't live to be twenty!"

"Wait a minute!" David protested. "I'm the quiet one! I like to read. But you people collect trouble like honey collects flies! I'll be surprised if I survive the summer!"

They argued amiably as the taxi sped them swiftly toward the Rhine River and the home of Herr and Frau Kuli. The Kulis were Mr. Daring's friends and the three would stay at their home for the days they were in Düsseldorf.

Mark and David were each seventeen years old. Mark was five feet, eleven inches tall, thickset and powerfully muscled. He had blond hair like his father, and a friendly face that often concealed his sharp intelligence.

David had dark hair, was two inches taller than Mark, broad shouldered, and lean. He, too, was strong through consistent training and exercise.

Sixteen-year-old Penny was five feet seven inches, slender, with light brown hair and, as David observed often, deep brown eyes. She was a serious photographer.

Mr. Daring had sent them to Düsseldorf, Germany, to meet a group from the French-German business coalition that backed his project in Egypt. The three were to explain privately the nature of the opposition they'd encountered from gangs directed by the former East German secret police, and Mr. Daring's plans for overcoming these difficulties. Because of the great amount of money involved in the project, secrecy and proper security measures were essential.

Already in Egypt and in France, elements from the former East German secret police had tried to steal information from Daring's office concerning an ancient Egyptian tomb his men had discovered buried in the sand.

"Kids, I need your help," Daring had told them at the end of their visit to Athens. "I'd like for you three to go ahead of me to Düsseldorf and brief Heinrich Kuli, the head of the German unit we're working with. He and his wife want you to stay with them while you're there. Then you can meet Carolyn and me back in Paris. I want you to take him our new encrypted phone and some diskettes with project data. After all that's happened lately, I can't trust this to the delivery services."

The three were excited at being sent off to Germany on their own, and anxious to meet Heinrich Kuli. Mr. Daring wanted them to explain to him the dangers they'd encountered with the enemies who'd made such desperate efforts to sabotage Daring's project and steal the vast amounts of money they hoped to realize.

As the taxi drove them through the outskirts of Düsseldorf, toward Heinrich Kuli's home on the Rhine, David asked the driver about the news reports he'd read concerning the neo-Nazi groups in Germany. The driver knew no English, so David had to translate his conversation for Mark and Penny.

"He says that there's been a lot of neo-Nazi activity since the reunion with East Germany. Some people in West Germany resent the money the union has cost their economy, and this has given the small group of neo-Nazis a chance to cause trouble."

"Are those the people they call 'skinheads'?" Mark asked.

"That's right," David replied. "They shave their heads and wear a kind of uniform and use a lot of Nazi symbols."

The driver told David more about the group, and David translated for Mark. "There was an explosion last night in a government building, he says. Some files were taken and a swastika was sprayed on the floor of the room. The police won't say what information the files contained, but the news media speculate that the neo-Nazis will use it to hurt the government."

"There's the Rhine!" David said suddenly, pointing out the window. "We're almost there."

"I didn't know it was so wide!" Mark exclaimed in surprise.

"It's not that wide everywhere," David answered.

"But here it's almost a thousand feet across. And the current is fast."

Then the cab pulled up to the curb. David paid the driver, and the three took their bags and looked at the boats on the river.

"There's a lot of traffic on this water," David said. "Barges and freight, and lots of tour boats."

Then they turned to the house behind them, walked through a gate, past a low wall decked with flowering bushes, and rang the bell.

Frau Kuli was tall, with gray hair and bright blue eyes that twinkled with pleasure as she shook their hands. "Welcome, welcome. We've been expecting you." She took them in and led them to the upstairs rooms where they'd be staying.

"Unpack your things while I make some hot chocolate and find some cake," she said.

Good as her word, she soon had them feasting in the sun room, with its wide windows that faced the Rhine. The Americans were fascinated with the constant parade of boats going up and down the important river. Frau Kuli's English was excellent, and they soon felt very much at home.

"My husband would like for you to come to his office as soon as you feel rested," she told them.

"We're ready now," David said. "Thanks for letting us stay here."

"It's our pleasure, David. Mark and Penny's father has stayed with us before, and we're glad that you three could come in his place."

Mark went up to the room and retrieved a briefcase from his luggage. Then Frau Kuli drove them downtown to her husband's office. The three were surprised to see lovely residential districts so close to the city's center, and asked Frau Kuli about it.

"Many German cities are like this," she explained. "That makes it possible for school children to come home to lunch with their mothers and fathers. It also makes it easy for many of us to shop."

She pulled up at the curb and showed them her husband's office.

"Just go up those steps and ring the bell," she told them. "The secretary will let you in."

They thanked her as they got out. She drove away, and they walked toward the stairs. At the top, David pointed to his right. "There they are—skinheads!"

Mark and Penny looked in the direction David indicated. There, half a dozen scruffy looking youths in jeans and black jackets, with shaved heads, swaggered along the sidewalk, forcing pedestrians to make way before them.

"There are groups like that all over Germany," David said. "They're a small minority, and most Germans despise them. But they make a lot of trouble. Naturally, the news media give them a lot of coverage and blow their influence out of all proportion."

"Just like our media in the United States," Mark observed.

"Just like ours," David agreed.

David rang the bell. A pleasant-looking woman opened the door and David told her who they were.

"Mr. Kuli is expecting you," she smiled, speaking perfect English with a British accent. "Follow me."

Heinrich Kuli was a tall, distinguished-looking man with thick gray hair and a powerful frame. He greeted them warmly and ushered them into his office, waving them to thick, comfortable chairs. After asking about Mark and Penny's father, he got down to business.

"Well, Mark, your father tells me that you three will fill me in on the difficulties the company has encountered. Go ahead."

"Yes, sir," Mark replied. He told of the trouble with the mining rights in East Africa, and of the gang of thieves led by former East German secret police. "Their leader's name is Hoffmann," he said.

"Your father told me about Hoffmann, Mark. But I thought his gang was broken up in Paris a couple of weeks ago. Did he get away?"

"Yes, sir, he did. He had a spy in Dad's firm in Africa, and that man learned a lot. He learned about the project in Egypt. They almost got away with a tremendous treasure."

"I know a little about that, too," Kuli said. "Your father told me that the three of you had something to do with foiling them there, didn't you?"

"Yes, sir, we did," Mark said. "And Mr. Froede. He's the one who got the police. That's when the

Egyptian government caught a lot of them. But Hoffmann followed Dad to Paris and tried to steal information there."

"He almost did, too," David added. "That's why Mr. Daring wants you to use a coded telephone when you talk with him. It's in Mark's case. Mr. Daring's got a phone just like it, and so does Mr. Froede in Cairo."

"Dad says you can talk safely on this phone," Mark continued. "Keno's got one, too, and he's still in Paris. The French group will keep his phone when he goes back to Egypt, so you and they can talk with each other, and with Dad and Mr. Froede in Egypt. Hoffmann's gang won't be able to listen in."

"Actually, Mark," David corrected, "they can listen in. They just can't *understand* what they hear."

"That's right," Mark admitted with a grin. "The phone's a new digital model. It's coded with an algorithmic formula that adds too many digits for ordinary machines to decipher. But Dad wants you to know that Hoffmann's gang is ex-STASI. That means they've got the KGB behind them. So they've got the best equipment in the world, and could ultimately break most any code."

"I understand that, Mark," Kuli said with a broad smile, "but this should do us for the near future. And that's all we need."

He was silent a moment. Then he shook his head as if at a puzzle. "Ex-STASI! One of the most vicious police organizations on earth! The East German equivalent of the Russian KGB! The news media would have us believe that they're tame now, all dismantled since the reunion of the two *Germanys*!" He shook his head again. "What fools in the press, to believe that so many men with guns and power will so easily lay them down!"

He stood up and paced the room. "But at least they're restrained now. And some are in jail. Others are out of work. But those people are dangerous, too. And their budgets have been cut badly. That's why they've tried to steal mines and treasures and anything they can get their hands on!"

Stopping before them, he said, "Well, my wife and I are glad you're here! I want you to come with me each morning to the office, and work with me. We'll study the papers you've brought, and you can fill me in on your father's plans. In the afternoons, we want you to see the sights in Düsseldorf."

He handed David a folded map. "Take this afternoon to explore our city. Here's a guidebook as well. There's a lot to see here, and we want you to enjoy your visit. I'll meet you back at the house for dinner. We eat at 7:30."

CHAPTER 2

SKINHEADS!

Mark, David, and Penny were having a great time. They'd spent an hour wandering around the open market in the center of the city. Rows and rows of carts and booths held food and all kinds of goods for people to buy. They'd wandered past these, looking at all the things being sold, watching the crowds of people from all over Germany and beyond.

"I can't get over the beautiful flowers everywhere!" Penny exclaimed. "They're in window boxes of homes and businesses all over the city! Germans love flowers, don't they?"

"They sure do," David agreed. "Almost everyone grows them in their yards. That's what makes German towns so colorful, even in the winter."

"They love dogs, too," Mark said. "Look at all the dogs on leashes."

They stopped at an outdoor restaurant for lunch. Here they studied the map and guidebook Herr Kuli had given them. "There's an old Protestant church hidden behind a wall," David noted. "Protestants were a minority in this part of Germany, and in times past they

15

had to hide their church buildings behind walls so people couldn't see them from the streets."

Just then two soldiers went by, and Mark asked in surprise, "Are those British uniforms?"

"I bet they are," David replied. "Düsseldorf was a headquarters for the British army of occupation after the Second World War. I think those are from the English Army of the Rhine, which is part of the NATO force."

"Let's see some more of the city," Mark said. They got up and began wandering through the streets, checking their path by the map as they strolled through the fascinating city. David translated signs for Mark and Penny as they passed shop windows and stores of every kind. Occasionally Penny stopped to take pictures.

After a while they came to a narrow street. "This looks old," David said.

"Let's go down it!" Penny said, excited. "I see some old houses; they'd make great pictures."

The constricted passage twisted to their left. Compared with the crowds they'd seen around the market and the city's shops, this road was almost deserted.

Suddenly they heard cries from a narrow alley to their right. Startled, they stopped and looked.

"There's a gang beating up someone on the ground! He needs help!" Mark said.

"Let's go!" David said at once.

"Penny, use your telephoto lens and take their picture!" Mark said as he began to run. "But stay here and call for police if we need help!"

Mark and David dashed down the street toward the struggling group. One boy on the ground, was being kicked by a skinhead, while another boy held down on his knees by a large man was being beaten by a third skinhead. A fourth stood watching.

"Now!" Mark yelled as they got close. The skinhead beating the kneeling youth looked up in surprise, just in time to receive Mark's thick fist in his face. He fell back to the ground, stunned. The big man holding the victim, jumped up with a snarl. Instantly Mark spun on his foot and delivered a powerful kick to the man's stomach. The skinhead doubled over and collapsed to the street.

David, meanwhile, ran straight for a heavy man who'd whirled at Mark's yell. He drove his right fist into the man's nose, then slammed his other into his stomach. The man fell backward, doubled over, and collapsed.

The fourth skinhead saw his comrades fall, whirled around, and raced away. The three injured men moaned on the ground.

"Let's get these boys out of here," Mark said, helping one of the groaning youths to his feet. David helped the other, and they went back to the main street as fast as the injured boys could move.

The boy's faces were bruised. One held his injured arm, the other limped painfully. But they could walk.

They stammered their thanks to the two Americans,

and were visibly surprised when David replied in fluent German. But, like so many Europeans, they were anxious to practice the English they'd studied in school.

"What happened?" David asked the boy he was helping.

"Those are Nazis," he replied. "They caught us at a bookstore. I'd just bought a book written in English. They called us traitors to our country. They followed us and dragged us down that street."

Mark and David kept looking behind them, but it was obvious that those skinheads weren't going to pursue them.

"Let's slow down, Mark," David said. "They're not following."

"That was wonderful!" Penny exclaimed as they drew near. "And I got their pictures! I got all their faces!"

"You guys break anything?" Mark asked.

The German boys said that there were no broken bones, just bruised muscles.

"I think they would have hurt us badly if you hadn't come, though," the tall one said.

Gradually the sense of danger passed. The tall boy who had a limp was Karl, he told them. His brother, Willi, was shorter. Karl was fifteen, Willie fourteen. They lived with their mother. "Our father left us four years ago," Karl said sadly.

"Let's get something to eat," Mark suggested, as they came to a sidewalk cafe.

"We don't have any money," Karl said apologetically.

"You don't need any," Mark replied. "David's loaded with cash! We'll let him pay."

The German boys protested, but Mark insisted. "Look, we rescued you! That makes you our prisoners, right?" He grinned at them.

The German boys laughed at this, and agreed to be David's guests.

They sat down, and David told them, "Order what you want. We feed our prisoners well."

When the waitress came, Kurt and Willi smiled, but only ordered hot chocolate.

"That's not enough," David protested. "Order something to eat!"

But Karl and Willi were too embarrassed to order.

"These guys are thin, Mark," David said. "They need nourishment if they want to make it home. I'll order some sausages."

So David ordered sausages and brown bread for them all, hoping to fill up the too-thin German boys. Karl and Willi were neatly dressed, but their clothes were not new. It was obvious their mother didn't have a lot of money.

When the food came, the boys waited a moment, looking at each other. "Let's thank the Lord," David said. And he did, giving thanks for the food and for the fact that they were all safe.

Karl and Willi beamed as they looked at their new friends. "Then you are Catholic also?" Willi asked.

"Actually, we're Protestants," Penny said. "But

we're Christians, which is what matters more."

"We don't know a lot of Protestants," Karl said carefully. He tried to hide his disappointment. "We believe
that Protestants think differently than we do." He
stopped, embarrassed, clearly not wishing to offend
their rescuers.

"Well, there are real differences," David agreed.
"But we believe in the Father, Son, and Holy Spirit.
And we believe He's one God. That's what you
believe, isn't it?"

"Yes," they both agreed.

"And we believe that God became a man in Jesus
Christ, to suffer His own judgment for our sins. And
you believe that, I think."

"Yes, we do," Karl agreed.

"Well, let's thank God for the things we *agree*
about!" Mark laughed. "Like, the fact that your German
chefs really know how to make good sausage!"

They all laughed. And this is how Mark and David
and Penny began one of the more interesting afternoons of their lives. The two German boys were
fascinating and knowledgeable companions. As an
added bonus and to the Americans' delight, they knew
classical music and loved it.

When they'd finished their snack, the five wandered
around the central part of Düsseldorf and then along
the elegant Königsallee. This wide boulevard ran along
both sides of the old town moat and was lined with
shops and businesses, restaurants and cafes. Karl and

Willi pointed out some of the interesting landmarks, then took them to a bookstore.

"There's lots of English books here," Karl told them.

Soon, each of them was deeply engrossed in a book. Penny stopped at the section on photography, while Mark and Willi picked up books on naval warfare.

David went to a section with books on history. Struck by the painting of an armored knight on the cover of one volume, David picked it up. He leafed through the book with growing excitement. When he came to a chapter describing the knighting ceremony used by German Military Orders in the Middle Ages, he couldn't keep it to himself.

"Look at this," he said, taking the book to where to Mark and Willi were reading. The three looked at a picture of a young German knight kneeling before an altar. They then read about the training he'd had, the fighting skills he'd developed, and the ceremony in which he dedicated himself to God as a soldier to protect pilgrims who visited the Holy Lands.

"They made vows to God," David pointed out, "to live and die as Christian soldiers, giving their lives for others."

"My mother told us about that," Karl said, his face solemn. "When my father left us, she told us we could grow up to be faithful men who would keep their vows to their wives and children. That's what we're going to do."

"That's what our dads tell us," David said. "But we

haven't had knights in our history like you two have."
David loved to study German history, and had learned
a lot about that people's past.

David wondered how this fact of German history
could be used to encourage Karl and Willi. His father
had often told him that in almost every country and
culture there were evidences of God's work, and prin-
ciples and practices that were admirable and noble.

Suddenly Karl glanced at his watch. "It's later than I
thought! We've got to leave! Our mother expects us
home!"

Willi said, "Why don't you come home with us and
meet her?"

"Oh, I'd love to do that!" Penny said. "Can we?"

"We don't have to be at the Kulis' until 7:30,"
David said to Mark. "Why not?"

"Let's go!" Mark said.

Later that evening, as they ate dinner with the Kulis,
the three Americans told of their encounter with the
German boys and the fight with the skinheads.

"I'm glad you rescued them," Herr Kuli said.
"Those skinheads often beat up on people. And a lot of
the time they get away with it. Many people are too
afraid of them to call the police."

"They didn't get away with it today!" Penny said
firmly. "Mark and David knocked three of them down,
and the other one ran away! They'll be more cautious
in the future!" She smiled at the boys, pride showing in

her eyes.

"Penny took their pictures, Herr Kuli," David said. "She got them actually beating up those boys. Wouldn't the police be interested in these shots?"

"They sure would! That's wonderful, Penny! Let me have that film and I'll take it to the police in the morning."

"Just be careful not to run into them again," Mrs. Kuli said anxiously.

"We'll be careful," David said. Then he turned to her husband. "Herr Kuli, those boys were thin. We met their mother, and she's very nice. She works in a shop, but doesn't make much money. But the boys ought to get some training in body building, and in self-defense."

"Not many of our young men do that, David," their host replied. "They're not like you Americans."

"But just some weights and a book of instructions would build those boys up. They'd see the difference in half a year. In one year they'd be a lot stronger than they are now! And a good school of karate would teach them how to defend themselves."

"Well, I know there are schools of judo and karate here," Herr Kuli replied. "In fact, a friend of mine, a grocer, is a student in one of them. Let me talk to him. He's of their faith and I'm sure he'd be interested in helping those two boys."

David and Mark were elated at the thought that Karl and Willi might get some training and skill in defending themselves.

"I'll call after dinner, and see what I can find out," Herr Kuli said. "Then, which of you boys plans to challenge me to a game of chess?"

"Mark's pretty good, sir," David said. "Sometimes he beats his dad."

"Excellent! You can set up the board, Mark, while I call Herr Conrad."

That night, Mark and David read their Bibles before turning out the light. When they'd finished, they talked for a while about the day's events.

"Boy!" David exclaimed, "imagine if Herr Kuli can get his friend to take an interest in Karl and Willi!

"I hope they'll be willing to go with him to karate school." Mark said. "Remember how hard it was for us to pay for their sausages!"

"But he could give them work. That way, they'd be earning their lessons."

"They'd also have a man to spend time with them," Mark added.

"And they'd get a lot of self-confidence as they trained! They wouldn't have to fear those skinheads."

They turned out the lights, thankful for Herr Kuli and his friend and their interest in two boys who had no father to look after them.

After a few moments, David spoke again. "The Bible says that God is the father of the fatherless, and this proves it!"

Mark would have agreed, if he hadn't already fallen asleep.

CHAPTER 3

BLACKMAIL

Herr Dantzler was so deeply asleep that he didn't hear the phone until the fourth ring. His wife, recovering from a bout of asthma, was in the guest bedroom. There was no phone there, so she didn't hear the ringing at all.

Groggily, he switched on the light and reached for the instrument.

"Ja?" he said, struggling to wake up.

"Herr Dantzler?" the voice on the phone inquired.

He didn't recognize the raspy voice, but as the man spoke, the threat was unmistakable. They had just found documentary evidence linking him with financial transactions that had benefited the former East German secret police, the voice informed him. Those files, taken from the blown-up safe in the government records building, had incriminated him and others. They would call him again later in the week. They expected him to cooperate. Or the information would be given to the police.

The phone went dead.

He was now wide awake, but in mental shock. What

files incriminated him? What would they want him to do?

But he knew the answers to those questions. He was president of the third largest bank in the city. And he knew that his bank had been used by the KGB and the STASI to transfer funds for their own purposes, using legitimate businesses as cover. Officers such as himself could be blackmailed for doing things they did not realize were actually serving the Communist cause. Then the Communists themselves would frame them! They would demand money. And he would have to give it to them. Or go to trial. And prison.

Herr Dantzler shivered. He slept no more that night.

The next morning, Herr Kuli drove Mark and David to his office, where the three spent four hours going over the papers Mr. Daring had sent. Penny planned to go shopping with Mrs. Kuli and join the boys later. Several times, Herr Kuli used the encoded phone to call Jim Daring in Paris. The boys got to speak with him also.

Later, after lunch, Herr Kuli took them to his friend's store. It was not far from Kuli's office, still in the central part of town. Herr Conrad was a short man, powerfully built, with thick black hair. He told them he was delighted at the thought of taking Karl and Willi to karate class with him and his son.

"Bring them by later this afternoon, and I'll talk with them. If they're interested, I'll have my wife give their mother a call. We'll go meet her so she'll know who her sons will be with. I can give them work so that they can pay for their lessons."

This pleased them all, and they promised to bring Karl and Willi around to the store when they met them in a couple of hours.

And this is what they did. The two German boys were awed at the thought of the training Herr Conrad proposed, but expressed doubts that they could do it. He pointed to the two Americans and told them, "You boys could be strong like these two in a couple of years. And you could defend yourselves like they do, too. It just takes training. Think how you'd feel, knowing you could take care of yourselves and your mother."

The thin boys looked at each other, genuinely interested now.

Penny went with them when Herr Conrad took the boys to his karate school. His twelve-year-old son, Hans, joined them there. Hans was a slender boy, not large, and the German boys wondered how he could handle himself in a karate school. But when they saw him train, they knew how fast and skilled he was! Karl asked David about this.

"Strength helps," David said, "but the main thing is skill. Skill comes from serious training. If you really want to be good at this, you can do it. Watch how the instructor trains the class."

There were about a dozen men and boys in the class. Herr Conrad had introduced Mark and David to the instructor, who had invited the Americans to join in the training. Karl and Willi watched, fascinated, as the instructor led the careful warm-up period—the calisthenics, the slow, practiced moves. Then they saw the carefully controlled sparring, as different men and boys were matched against each other.

Herr Kuli pointed out the care with which the more skilled men and boys sparred with those who had less skill. "It's part of the code. The good students are very careful with those who are not so good. They're careful to train them, but not to hurt them. That way, newcomers learn gradually and safely."

David and Mark had not had consistent exercise the past several weeks because of their adventures and travels. They loved participating in the class.

But, as they walked out of the gym, they both knew they'd be feeling the effects the next day!

"Gosh, it feels great to train again!" David said. "But am I worn out!"

"Me, too!" Mark agreed. "What a teacher that man is! He really gave us a workout!"

"And he runs a tight ship, too," David said. "He doesn't allow any foolishness or careless fighting. It's a really safe place to train and learn the sport."

"That's what Herr Conrad told Willi and Karl's mother," Mark replied. "That's why she agreed to let them go. Gosh, that'll change their lives in a year! You know, David, if all we do on this trip to Germany is plug those boys into Herr Conrad and the karate school, it'll sure be worth it."

"It sure will. I just hope they can avoid those skin-heads for a while until they learn how to defend themselves."

That night after supper, Herr Kuli took Mark, Penny, and David into his study. His face was very serious, and they knew something was up.

"Did you hear the news about the explosion in the government office?"

"We heard that it happened," David said, "but we don't know anything about it."

"Well, a safe was blown and files were stolen. A swastika was sprayed on the floor where the robbery occurred, to make it look like the work of neo-Nazis. And that's who the news media are blaming, so that's what everyone believes. But it's a lie. A cover-up, in fact."

"Then who was behind it, Herr Kuli?" Penny asked.

"I got a call from a friend today. He said he had to meet me away from his office. He's one of the most prominent men in Düsseldorf, and he's very scared. After we talked, I called your father on the encrypted phone. And he put me in touch with his friend, Henri, in French security."

"He's a great guy!" Mark said fervently, remembering the man's fighting prowess and how he'd helped Mark fight off the gang that tried to kidnap Penny in the Paris catacombs.

"That's what your father says. Henri told me that

French intelligence thought the robbery might not be connected with the Nazis at all. They think that's just a cover for another group, the same group you boys had trouble with. Henri's contact in German security had already called him about that exploded safe. The French and German police stay in close touch, he told me, particularly in matters relating to the Soviet espionage network and the different Eastern European spy systems. He warned me to be alert. And asked me to warn you also."

"Is that who they think is behind the explosion in that office?" David asked.

"That's what they suspect, David," Herr Kuli replied.

This was sobering news. The teenagers were quiet for a moment.

Then Penny asked, "Does Henri think that those people know about you and your work with dad and his company?"

"He's not sure. But they are after money! And my friend, the man who came to see me today, can get it for them if he's forced." Herr Kuli was silent for a moment, gathering his thoughts. "What I'm going to say must be kept secret. My friend is being blackmailed. People have evidence against him that they claim could put him in prison. But he doesn't want to cooperate with them. He wants them caught, even if he himself has to go to trial. He's the president of one of the banks that is financing our work in Egypt. He needs our help. And he needs it badly."

"What can we do, Herr Kuli?" Mark asked.

Herr Kuli leaned forward before he spoke. "I don't want to put you three in danger. But you can help. My friend needs someone to act as a courier for him. He's got documents that can incriminate the people who are blackmailing him. They don't know this. He can't let any of his staff handle it. And he doesn't dare go to the police, or he might be killed on the way. But he wants to get these documents to me."

"We'll do anything we can to help," David said.

"Thank you," Herr Kuli said with a grateful smile. His face grew solemn again. "This is a very serious matter," he continued, choosing his words carefully. "Lives are at stake. And we can use your help. "I'm going to help my friend because he's willing to stand up to this blackmail. He's willing to risk his life to give the police evidence against those evil men.

"Incidentally, Penny, the police are very grateful for those pictures! They'll return your film tomorrow. They're going to pick up that gang you photographed— you got them in the actual act of beating up those two boys! That was great work!"

Penny smiled with pleasure at the compliment. "I'm so glad I could help. Maybe those neo-Nazis will be kept in jail for a while!"

"Let's hope so!" Herr Kuli said. Then he told them of Herr Dantzler. "He's a man in high office and he has a family. He's an honest man. But his bank was used by cover groups to handle funds for the KGB and the STASI. Many banks and businesses were used this way—in fact, they're *still* being used—without their knowing it. Then the Communists suddenly show up and threaten to give evidence to the police if people don't cooperate with them."

"And is that the kind of information somebody took from that safe they exploded?" David asked.

"That's right," Herr Kuli said. "But Herr Dantzler has been able to gather a lot of information about the STASI. Let me tell you what you can do to help Herr Dantzler."

CHAPTER 4

HOFFMANN'S PLAN

The trim blond man was in complete control of the meeting. It was a strangely mixed crowd seated before him. Four men in business suits sat in chairs along one wall. Opposite them were five skinheads in black jackets and trousers. Their shaved heads and grubby black clothes contrasted strangely with the well-dressed businessmen. Almost all the men were smoking. The room was adequately, but not luxuriously, furnished: a desk, two sofas, half a dozen chairs. The walls were bare.

Hoffmann stood behind the desk and surveyed the waiting men. Then he coughed. He hated cigarette smoke, but he said nothing to this group. He was in charge, but he was new. He wanted their confidence.

"The first part of the plan went like clockwork," he said proudly. "Herr Heller here," he nodded to the businessman at his left, "delivered the plastic explosive to our man in the government records building."

No one would have recognized the well-dressed Fritz as the man who'd fired the crossbow across the street two nights before. He removed the elegant black and ivory cigarette holder from his thin lips and nodded slightly. The others held him in obvious respect.

"Manfred delivered the message to our bank president," Hoffmann continued. The eyes of the men turned to the smallest skinhead. He didn't blink. The men looked away. Evil exuded from the silent man like morning fog from a lake.

"Manfred will call the bank president again tonight. He'll tell him the schedule of payments, and the banks to which the money must be sent. The payments will be in cash at each bank."

"But even the president can't wire off that much cash," one of the businessmen objected. "How can we get all the money you say we need?"

"Herr Dantzler will manage to do it," Hoffmann said curtly. "He understands the consequences to himself if he fails to do as we command."

Hoffmann surveyed the men in the room. Then he continued. "The money will be wired to accounts in Paris, Frankfurt, and Bern. Our people will appear at once to pick up the money at each place. We don't want any delays or time for bank officials to question these orders for cash. These three withdrawals will secure the money we need. We've promised Herr Dantzler that we'll help him escape after he robs his own bank." Hoffmann smiled thinly.

The men smiled back. Did Herr Dantzler *really* think they would let him get away? Every man in the room knew that they couldn't afford to let him live.

The jangling of the phone suddenly interrupted the stillness of the room. The men stiffened, all except Hoffmann. Supremely confident, in complete command, he picked up the phone. "Ja?" He listened for a moment, acknowledged, and hung up. For a minute he said nothing. He was visibly angry.

"Three American teenagers have gotten in our way several times this summer," he said finally. "They just happened to be in the wrong place at the wrong time, and they've caused us to lose millions of dollars!"

"What do the Americans have to do with us?" the largest skinhead asked contemptuously. He wasn't in the least interested in Hoffmann's previous failures. He just wanted to be sure the blond man wouldn't botch the job they were on now.

Hoffmann glared at the man. "Just this. Those three are here in Düsseldorf now. It's uncanny! They're with a man whose firm is part of the business coalition we're trying to rob."

"What are American kids doing here?" the skinhead insisted.

"They work for Daring, an American engineer. He's the father of two of them. His company is working on a giant project with a French-German firm, and he uses the three of them as messengers. We don't know why he sent them to Düsseldorf. But they could cause us trouble." He paused in thought.

The men in the room looked at each other. How

could the deadly Hoffmann be troubled by three American teenagers? They'd all noticed the scars on his face, and they'd heard he'd had several misfortunes that summer. Had those kids shaken his nerve?

"I wonder if those were the kids who broke up one of our gangs yesterday," Manfred said thoughtfully. He stubbed out his cigarette and lit another.

"We sent gangs into the city to make trouble and attract attention, as you ordered, Hoffmann. And we contacted our friends in the media to cover these gangs. Naturally they did, giving us major time on the evening news. This smoke screen worked, because now everyone believes that neo-Nazi gangs were behind the robbery of the government files."

"I still don't understand what have the Americans to do with this." one of the men said irritably.

"They jumped one of our gangs," Manfred replied. "Our men were beating up two German boys, and these Americans surprised them. Three of our men were hurt."

He glared around the room. "Not only that, the girl photographed our men during the fight and three of them were picked up by the police this morning."

They were all shocked at this news. The police were already involved! The men threw nervous glances at each other.

"Those American boys can fight," Hoffmann continued. "They're not to be taken lightly. But we can't let them get in our way now!"

He sketched out the plan. "Manfred will call Herr

Dantzler again with final instructions. He'll remind him of our promise to help him get out of Germany." Hoffmann smiled again, and the men smiled in return.

"Meanwhile, Fritz will arrange to meet Dantzler and explain how we'll help him escape. He'll also receive from Dantzler the cash he's promised to withdraw. Dantzler will trust Fritz more than he will you men with no hair."

Everyone smiled at that.

"How much money will we get altogether?" one of the businessmen asked.

Hoffmann paused. "About six million deutsche marks," he answered finally.

They were impressed.

Hoffmann continued. "That will enable us to continue financing some of our espionage networks throughout Eastern Europe. We've got to maintain these networks, and we've got to be patient. Eastern Europe's attempts to imitate the capitalist West will fail. That will be our chance to recover power."

"So Herr Dantzler is the key?" one of the businessmen asked.

"Herr Dantzler is a key to this operation," Hoffman replied. "We've got others planned."

"And he will deliver this money by wiring the banks in Paris and Bern and Frankfurt?"

"He will. He'll send out cash orders to each of these cities simultaneously. The whole deal will be finished by tomorrow afternoon." Hoffmann was lost in thought. Clearly, another idea had entered his mind. Finally, he voiced it. "It just occurred to me that if we could capture one of those American kids, Daring's firm would have to cough up a handsome ransom to get the kid back. We could make a double killing."

Manfred spoke quickly. "My men would be delighted to revenge themselves on those Americans. They'll beat them to a pulp!"

Hoffmann regarded him thoughtfully. "Let's plan on it, then. We know where they're staying—at Herr Kuli's home. They work with him in the mornings, then wander around the city in the afternoons. It shouldn't be hard to pick up one of them."

"My men will take care of it," Manfred said grimly, stubbing out his cigarette viciously.

Hoffmann smiled.

CHAPTER 5

INCRIMINATING INFORMATION!

The secretary ushered David, Penny, and Mark into the office of the bank's president. She was clearly surprised that these young strangers would be given an appointment by such a distinguished businessman, and she moved slowly as she left the room, anxious to hear as much as she could.

"Sit down, friends, sit down," Herr Dantzler said cordially. "I've received your father's message, and I'll be happy to listen to his proposal."

Reassured by these words, the secretary closed the door. *So it was a legitimate business meeting, she thought. Nothing unusual to report to her real boss.*

The three teenagers sat down in the luxurious chairs before Herr Dantzler's desk and he chatted with them in a friendly way for a few minutes. David was amazed that Herr Dantzler could appear so calm. No one would suspect that he was being threatened with prison by blackmailers; nor that to escape that fate, he would have to steal monstrous sums from his own bank and thus be a fugitive of the law.

Dantzler was not tall. His stocky frame was topped by a completely bald head. Bright blue eyes looked searchingly through thick glasses in dark plastic frames. There was a thin scar over his right eye, David noticed. His English was excellent, but his accent was very thick.

"Tell me about your father's plans," he said to Mark.

Mark went into the speech Herr Kuli had sketched out for him. "Well, sir, Dad's firm is working for a French-German company that's beginning a big project in Egypt. As you know, Herr Kuli's firm is working with Dad, and he asked me to bring you the latest proposal they want you to help finance."

"Let me see the papers, please," Dantzler asked.

Mark walked over to the desk, reached across, and handed the banker the large sealed envelope he'd brought with him. At the same time, Herr Dantzler slipped into Mark's hand a small square package wrapped in brown paper. Mark casually rested his hand on the desk, with the brown package concealed underneath. Then he turned and sauntered back to his chair, slipping the package into his pocket.

Herr Kuli had warned the three Americans that Dantzler's actions could well be under the surveillance of a hidden TV camera. He'd also told them that their conversation in the banker's office would most likely be recorded. He hadn't told them how he and Dantzler had worked out this plan without being overheard, and they hadn't asked. He'd only warned them to say nothing that might incriminate the bank president.

Opening the large envelope that Mark had handed him, Herr Dantzler took out the pages and began to scan them, reading very rapidly. *He's speed-reading,* David thought to himself. This interested David because his father had trained him to read rapidly also. "It will save years of your life for other things," he'd told David often. Mark and Penny had had the same training.

The three waited patiently while Dantzler read.

In a few minutes he looked up. "Excellent, excellent! I'm sure we can increase Herr Kuli's credit by the amount he requests. These figures are very persuasive! He's always been one of our most reliable customers."

They all began to realize that he was speaking in a loud voice, as if he wished to be heard by eavesdroppers. They all began to admire the banker's courage.

Dantzler looked suddenly at his watch. "It's noon!" he said. "Have you eaten lunch yet?"

"No, sir," David replied.

"Neither have I. How would you like to be my guests at an excellent restaurant where I dine at least once a week? My assistant will look at these papers, and have something ready for you to take back to Herr Kuli when we return."

They readily agreed to this. Herr Dantzler excused himself while he took the envelope to the office of his assistant. He returned in a few minutes. "Let's go!"

They walked out of the bank, turned to their left,

and strolled along the street. Herr Dantzler began telling them about Düsseldorf and its history, pointing out offices of major businesses as they walked past. His guests began to get a sense of the financial importance of this great German city.

"Düsseldorf is called the 'Paris of Germany,' " he told them, with obvious pride. "There are very important trade fairs here each year. Our airport is first class, and we're really a center of international commerce. Düsseldorf's position on the Rhine River has made the city a commercial power for centuries."

David, Penny, and Mark were struck by the variety of people they passed. Elegantly dressed men and women brushed past punkers and occasional skinheads. There were Japanese tourists, Turks, Arabs, Africans, Britons, and people from more countries than they could identify. All lived in and were a part of Düsseldorf's bustling life.

"Here's my favorite restaurant," Dantzler told them as he stopped and looked inside the long glass window. Then he frowned. "But it looks almost full!" He looked at them in apparent consternation. Then he made a decision: "Let's go to another one!"

Penny was surprised; half the tables were still empty! What did Herr Dantzler have in mind? She looked inquiringly at Mark and David. They, too, had noticed the empty tables.

Quickly Herr Dantzler turned to his left and led them down a narrow pedestrian lane. Turning again when they came to an intersection, he led them into a small restaurant in the middle of the block. Puzzled at his sudden change of plan and rapid pace, the Americans followed him into the darkened interior; once inside, it took their eyes several moments to adjust to the dim light. The place was filled with smoke.

"Here's a booth," Dantzler told them, pointing to an empty spot at the back of the room and leading them toward this. He waved Penny to a seat next to the wall, facing the door, then sat beside her. As David and Mark took their places opposite them, they saw that Herr Dantzler could watch the door from where he was sitting. Both boys were very alert.

As Herr Dantzler beckoned for the waiter, Mark and David exchanged glances. Both were thinking the same thought. Dantzler had very skillfully, and very naturally, led them to a different restaurant than the one he'd mentioned to his secretary. It had been very neatly done. If anyone had planned to eavesdrop on them during lunch, he would now have to change his plans quickly. If anyone had been able to follow them! The boys could see from Penny's eyes that she was thinking the same thing.

The waiter came and David ordered in German for Mark and Penny, knowing what they would enjoy. When the waiter left, Herr Dantzler became very serious.

"Let's use this time while we're still unobserved. Someone will follow us here soon enough! When we return to the office, I'll apologize, in the hearing of my secretary, for not taking you to the nice restaurant I'd first mentioned. But I knew they'd have someone waiting to listen to us there and that's why I brought you here."

Penny's eyes were wide. "Are you sure you're being followed, Herr Dantzler?" she asked, concern in her voice.

"I am sure, Penny," he replied. "But we have a few minutes now." He became very businesslike and looked directly at Mark. "First, that diskette I gave you, Mark, has a story on it, and I want Herr Kuli to get it. Something may happen to me, and the police would never get that information. They must have it!" His face was grim when he said this. Then he relaxed and laughed.

There was a mirror on the wall behind the booth, and David had been watching the door through this. That's how he noticed the tall man who entered the restaurant, stood stiffly for a moment in the door as his eyes adjusted to the dim light, and searched the tables with quick glances. He spotted Herr Dantzler and Penny, then looked away quickly and moved to a vacant seat at the bar. Sitting down, he studied the menu, pretending to ignore Dantzler and the Americans.

David was relieved that the man could not hear their conversation from where he sat.

"A man just came in and looked our way, Herr Dantzler," David said quietly. "He sat at the bar."

"I think he was looking at us," Penny added. She'd seen him also.

"Thank you," Dantzler replied. "I saw him, too. I'd better keep smiling as if we've got nothing to worry about. But I want you to tell Herr Kuli about this diskette. It has names on it, names of people I know to have been involved in the East German secret police." He paused. "Have you heard of the STASI?"

They told him that they had. For a moment his face was grim. "They're terrible. As brutal and ruthless as the Soviet KGB! They've been badly damaged since the reunion of the two Germanys, but they're still intact! They've still got their networks all over the world, certainly in united Germany. And they're using threats and blackmail to secure large sums of money to finance their continued espionage operations." He leaned forward. "And they're still being directed by the Soviet KGB! Your media is telling your people that eternal peace and utopia have arrived, that they can dismantle the American military and turn national attention to domestic issues. What lies!" He shook his head sadly. Then he brightened again. "I'll feel happier when you get that diskette to Herr Kuli. I describe some of the STASI contacts in the Soviet KGB, as well as their people in other banks in Western Europe. The information is vital! The police must have it!"

Then Dantzler changed the subject. He began to talk about his travels in the Soviet Union where he had been sent by his board of directors. "They wanted me to establish contacts with banks in the different Soviet republics. They had no idea at that time that those Republics would someday be free from Moscow's control! This has given us many business opportunities, and we're expanding our personnel and facilities to meet these opportunities."

The waiter brought them lunch, and as they ate they plied Dantzler with questions.

"Are Russians really free to start businesses of their own?" Mark asked him.

"Many of them are," Dantzler replied, "certainly more so than they were under communism. But they're starved for money with which to begin their work. They are starved also for the knowledge and skill to make independent decisions. For seventy years they've been told what to do by the central agencies in Moscow. And their dreadfully inefficient business policies have been subsidized by banks from the free nations of the world! Otherwise, that empire would have collapsed a half-century ago! "He looked sharply at the two boys across from him. "Did you know that American and Western European banks have financed the Soviet Union these past seventy years?"

Both boys nodded. "Yes, sir," Mark replied. "Our parents have told us that many times."

Dantzler shook his head. "Amazing," he said.

"Herr Dantzler," Penny said quietly, glancing again at the man who'd followed them, "I think that man at the bar just spoke into a small radio. He held it in his handkerchief, but I'm pretty sure that's what he was doing."

"I'm not surprised, Penny," Dantzler said. "He's reporting to his bosses. But what could be more innocent than our eating lunch in plain sight!"

The three couldn't help admiring the banker's calm courage.

"But we're almost through," Dantzler continued. "After we finish, we'll walk back to the office. My assistant will have the papers for you to take to Herr Kuli. Go at once to Kuli's office, and give him the diskette as well. Tell him I'll wait for his call."

The four finished lunch, and Herr Dantzler paid the waiter. They walked to the door without looking at the man sitting at the bar, and went into the street. On the way back to his office, Dantzler chatted as if he hadn't a care in the world.

As they walked through the door of the bank, Penny glanced backward. Five skinheads were loitering at the corner, looking toward them. She shivered and followed the men into the bank. In Herr Dantzler's office, a large envelope was waiting on the desk.

Dantzler picked this up. "Here's the report for Herr Kuli," he said smiling and handed it to Mark. "Tell him we are very grateful for his business, and that I will wait for his call to confirm the arrangement we've described in these documents." He ushered them to the door, shook their hands cordially, and went back to his office.

Mark, Penny, and David walked past the secretary's desk and toward the street entrance of the bank. Each was marveling at Herr Dantzler's courage.

CHAPTER 6

STALKED BY SKIN-HEADS!

I saw a gang of skinheads hanging around the corner when we went in," Penny said quietly as they walked out of the bank and stopped at the top of the steps.

"I saw them, too," David said.

"So did I," Mark replied. He looked to his left. "They're still there," he said. "And they're looking this way."

"Let's go right, then," David said quickly.

They walked down the steps to the broad sidewalk and turned right.

"Look for a taxi," Mark said as they walked rapidly along the sidewalk. However, there were so many pedestrians along this part of the sidewalk, they weren't able to go as fast as they would have liked.

At the corner, they turned. As they did so, David glanced back. The skinheads were following them and were not far behind! "They're coming this way," he said quietly.

The three quickened their pace as best they could

without giving the appearance of running away.

"We don't want them to think we noticed them," David said.

"Well, we don't know that they're following us," Mark said. "But we sure don't want to take a chance of being wrong. We've got to get Herr Dantzler's diskette to Herr Kuli."

"But surely they can't bother us on a main street," Penny said. "Not with so many people around."

"I hope you're right," Mark said fervently, remembering the skinheads who'd attacked the two German boys.

"I wish we could spot a policeman," David said, glancing around anxiously, hoping to see a uniform.

They came to a corner where pedestrians waited for the light to change. Now they were all getting nervous. Glancing back and up as if to view the tall building behind him, David saw that the gang of skinheads was much closer.

David laughed suddenly, pretending that Mark had just told a joke. He clapped his friend on the shoulder and pointed up to his right, as if the three of them were only sightseers having a good time. "Should I drop back and let you two get ahead? You're the one with the diskette, Mark, and we can't let those guys get that!"

"No!" Mark said at once. "We've got to stick together. I'm still looking for a taxi, but they're all full."

"Look!" Penny said suddenly. "There's a bridge over to our left. And there are more buildings that way.

We'd be in sight of a lot of people."

"Good for you, Penny," Mark said decisively. "Let's go!"

They turned left at once and walked with several other pedestrians across the street and onto the bridge that spanned the waterway in the middle of downtown Düsseldorf.

"How many skinheads do you see?" Mark asked as they hurried across.

"Five, I think," David replied. "And they're not the guys we jumped yesterday. These people are new."

"Wonder if they're all connected and work together." Mark said thoughtfully. "They might be coming after us because we beat up some of their friends yesterday."

This was an ominous thought and they all pondered it as they hurried along.

"You may be right," David said soberly. "We've got to stay with the crowds until we find a police officer, or a taxi."

But they saw no police as they walked rapidly along the street. Nor did they see a taxi that wasn't carrying passengers.

Now they were *really* nervous. "Could we go into this big department store?" Penny asked. "Surely they wouldn't attack us there!"

"Good idea," Mark agreed. They stepped quickly into the store, moved through a section filled with umbrellas of all kinds, then went around a wall that blocked their view of the street.

"Hey!" David said, grabbing Penny's arm. "See that sign? That's the way to the subway! Let's go down there before those guys come in!"

They went rapidly through this entrance and down the stairs. Here they came to the underground station. They had each bought a week's ticket the day before, so they didn't have to waste time at the ticket booth. Hurrying through the entrance they walked quickly to the train stop. They turned anxiously and scanned the platform behind them. Had the skinheads followed?

A train pulled in and began to let off passengers.

"Let's go!" David said.

The three dashed through the train doors just as they were closing.

"Did you see where this train is going?" Mark asked as they jammed themselves in and sat down across the aisle.

"No," David replied, eyes anxiously scanning the train platform to see if their pursuers were following. The train began to move.

"Oh! There they are!" Penny said, as the train left the station smoothly and gathered speed. "They just got to the bottom of the steps as we left. They must have seen us."

The three sank down in the seats, Penny and David in one, Mark facing them. Had the skinheads seen them?

"I guess they'll have to wait for the next train, at

least," Mark said hopefully. "That still gives us a good lead."

"Unless they've got a radio and can call their friends," David suggested. "That way they could have someone waiting for us at one of the next stops."

"Boy, if that's the case, we'd better get off as soon as we can!" Mark said at once.

The train pulled to a stop. Looking quickly around the station, the three saw only ordinary pedestrians.

"I don't see any skinheads," Penny said quietly as the doors opened. Some people got off, others got on.

"Let's go!" David said.

They moved quickly through the doors and onto the platform.

"Hey!" Mark said suddenly. "There's a train going back the way we came! Let's get on. We'll pass those guys and they won't know we've changed direction!"

They ran across the platform and dashed through the closing doors. Breathing sighs of relief, they sat down. Across the aisle, three teenagers in black pants and shirts stared at the Americans.

Mark tried to smile as he looked in Penny's eyes. "What a break finding this train! Those guys will pass us in a minute, going in the opposite direction!"

"Let's duck down when the train comes, so they can't see us," David suggested.

Just then the train roared by. They all ducked, pretending to tie their shoes, and waited a moment. Then they sat up again. Across the aisle from them, the

German teenagers looked puzzled at them with puzzled expressions.

"Whew!" Mark said gratefully, as he began to relax. "Now we've got some time to think what we're going to do."

"We've got to get this diskette to Herr Kuli," David said.

"But couldn't those men have radios?" Penny asked. "And couldn't their friends plan a trap for us outside Herr Kuli's office?"

This was a sobering thought. How could they reach Kuli to give him Dantzler's diskette?

"We can get off in a few stops and call him," David suggested. "He'll tell us how we can meet him."

The speeding train climbed out of the underground passage and slowed to a stop. The three Americans were very alert, looking carefully for signs of skinheads. The German teenagers across from them got up and left the train, and an elderly couple took their place. It seemed to take an eternity, but finally the train began to move again. They all breathed more easily.

"We've got to get off sometime and make that call," David said.

"Let's do it at the next stop," Mark replied.

Meanwhile, at Herr Dantzler's bank, a distinguished-looking man walked into the office. "I am Herr Heller," he announced to the receptionist. "Herr Dantzler is expecting me."

Lifting the phone, she informed Herr Dantzler, "Herr Heller is here to see you."

"Send him in," Herr Dantzler replied.

Dantzler himself opened the door and extended his hand to his visitor. "Come in, Herr Heller. What can I do for you?" Waving Heller to a seat, Dantzler sat down across from his visitor. Fritz Heller took out his cigarettes, placed one into a holder, and lit it. No one seeing him now, would have suspected that he was the Crossbowman who'd sent the explosives into the government office building.

"Is our conversation in this room secure?" he asked.

"Of course," Dantzler replied. So this was one of the men blackmailing him. His card indicated he was an officer in one of the international banks in Düsseldorf. Dantzler knew about Heller, although they'd never met before.

"Good," Heller said. "I am here to say that we appreciate your cooperation; and that we will see to it that you can escape without detection. Naturally, you will want to take enough money for yourself as you do so."

Dantzler's face was a mask. Did these men think for a minute that he trusted them to help him get away? They'd have to dispose of him, and he knew it. But he had to play along."Thank you," he replied.

Heller continued. "Tell me the arrangements for withdrawals."

Dantzler described the cash withdrawals he would make in two hours, and the instructions he'd prepared to fax to banks in Frankfurt, Germany; Paris, France; and Bern, Switzerland. He looked at his watch, then pointed to the fax machine on his desk. "Those instructions will be sent from my machine two hours from now, at 3:30. They will be acted upon at once. Your men must waste no time picking up the money. We can't take the chance of these instructions being detected by our bank's comptroller and canceled."

"No worry," Fritz Heller said. "Our men will arrive at exactly the time you've said and the money will be taken. Now, let me tell you how we'll get you and your wife out of Düsseldorf." He leaned forward and handed Dantzler a thick envelope. "You're going to Cairo. We've got a job for you there in an import-export firm. You'll never be found. With the cash you're withdrawing for yourself, and the salary from that job, you'll be comfortable for the rest of your life. Here's how we'll do this."

Dantzler played along—as if he believed every word the man said.

CHAPTER 7

"WHERE'S HERR KULI?"

Mark, Penny, and David left the train at the next stop. They stood on the platform for a long moment and looked carefully around, then walked quickly across the street.

"Let's get off this main road," David said. "We're too visible here!"

They walked down a side street, and at the end of that block found a public phone outside a small restaurant.

"I'll watch for skinheads while you call Herr Kuli," Mark said to David.

Quickly, David punched in the number to Kuli's office. Speaking rapid German, he talked to the secretary. As he hung up, Mark and Penny could tell from his face that something was wrong. "The secretary says that he's out of the office and won't be back for an hour."

This was bad news!

"We can't go to his office ourselves," David said,

"because those men are bound to be watching and they'd intercept us."

"That means we've got to stay out of sight until Herr Kuli gets back," Mark observed. "A lot could happen during that time. Boy! I feel like I'm carrying a ticking bomb! Herr Dantzler said that the police *had* to get this information as soon as possible so that they could arrest the men picking up the money! If only we knew whom we could contact in the police office-but we don't!"

"And the money's being wired to different countries!" David added. "Germany, France, and Switzerland! Even when the police get that diskette, they won't have much time to organize."

"Could we call Karl and Willi?" Penny asked. "They could meet us, and we could give the diskette to them. They could take it to Herr Kuli. No one would suspect them."

Mark frowned. "Gosh, I hate to get them involved in all this danger," he said.

"So do I," David responded, "but we may not have a choice. Penny's idea is a good one."

"Let's duck into that restaurant and think about it," Mark said. "We've got to get off the street and out of sight. If we can't reach Herr Kuli, we can call Karl and Willi."

"OK," David agreed. "We certainly can't stand around in the open like this. Everyone those skinheads are connected with will be looking for us."

The three paused a moment to scout the situation.

"See anyone around that looks suspicious?" David asked, glancing casually down the street. The three looked slowly around them. Two women were pushing baby carriages toward the restaurant, and some other people were walking away from them.

"They look harmless enough," Mark grinned. "Let's go in."

They entered the restaurant and stood for a moment, letting their eyes adjust to the dim light.

"There's a back booth," David said. They headed toward it. When the waiter came, David ordered hot chocolate for the three of them.

"Boy, what a mess!" Mark said, when the waiter had left. "I'm sure sorry you got mixed up in this, Penny!" He looked somberly into his sister's eyes.

"Me, too," David agreed. "These skinheads are trouble! And we don't have any idea how many of them are in this plot against Herr Dantzler and his bank!"

"Well, I certainly don't want you boys in danger by yourselves!" Penny said. "We've gotten out of tight spots before and we'll get out of this one, too."

"But it's Herr Kuli we've got to reach," David said. "I wonder where he is? His secretary wouldn't say."

At that moment, Herr Kuli was at the recently expanded Düsseldorf airport, greeting Mr. Daring, who'd just gotten off the plane from Paris.

"Welcome, Jim," Kuli said, gripping Daring's hand. "I'm glad you could come after all!"

"So am I!" Daring replied.

"This is a pleasant surprise! Until I got the fax from your office just an hour ago, I had no idea you were coming. Neither did your kids. In fact, they don't know yet!"

"Neither did I!" Daring laughed. "But my office in Cairo called early today. They've just discovered an extensive addition to the underground temple we're working on. This means more work for both your firm and mine! I brought all the data I could. Thanks for mobilizing so quickly."

"My office staff is ready, so let's get your luggage and be on our way." Herr Kuli led Daring to the luggage area where Daring retrieved his suitcases. Then they drove to Herr Kuli's office.

"Where are the kids?" Daring asked as the car moved swiftly through the city's traffic.

"They're visiting our banker, Herr Dantzler," Kuli replied. "His bank is one of those financing our work in Egypt, and the three of them are delivering some papers from my office." He looked over at Daring. "Have you talked with Henri today, Jim?" he asked quietly.

"No," Daring replied. "Anything new?" He was very alert.

"Yes. Things are moving rapidly. Too rapidly."

"What do you mean?" Daring asked.

"Dantzler's being threatened by a group of men who pretend to be neo-Nazis. Actually, Henri and our security police believe they're part of the same group of ex-STASI thugs who've been troubling you this summer."

"You mean Hoffmann's gang?" Daring asked, surprised. "I thought the French police had broken them up in Paris two weeks ago!"

"Henri told me that he'd thought so, too. But Hoffmann got away. And he and others have a scheme to rob Dantzler's bank. Dantzler's the bank president, and they're demanding money from him. They told him to wire cash orders to various banks in Western Europe. Their men will pick up the money at once, and Dantzler's bank will be robbed. They've offered to help him escape."

"He doesn't trust them, does he?" Daring asked at once.

"No, but he's on a tightrope. Mark and David and Penny went by his office to take our financial proposal. They're also going to pick up some information Dantzler has on the STASI group that's behind all this trouble. They're bringing it to my office. In fact, they're probably there now. We'll get this to the security police at once and they'll be able to grab Hoffmann's men as they pick up their money."

"What about Dantzler? Will he be jailed for this?"

"I hope not. The intelligence officer I talked with this morning said they think they can get him out of trouble if he makes it possible for them to arrest Hoffmann's men. There are so many of our people, Jim, who are being trapped and threatened with blackmail pressures like this, just because their businesses had connections with banks and merchants in Eastern Europe."

Kuli turned the car into the parking place by his office. The two men got out of the car and went into the building.

"Has David Curtis called?" Kuli asked his secretary as he approached her desk in the hall.

"Yes, sir, about an hour ago. I told him you'd be back later. But something's happened to our phone lines and we can't call out or receive calls."

"What?" Kuli said, stopping in his tracks and staring at her in surprise. "This isn't right!" He shot a troubled glance at Jim Daring.

The secretary spoke again. "This just happened thirty minutes ago. I'm expecting David to call back any minute."

"Where is he?" Kuli asked at once. "We'll call him."

"He didn't say. I could tell it was a public phone."

"Have you contacted the phone company about this?" he asked.

"Yes, sir, we called from the office next door. They said they'd work on it right away."

"Let me know as soon as we can use the phones," he said.

"Come into my office," Kuli said to Daring.

He closed the door behind him and waved Daring to a chair. "I don't understand this."

"Are the kids in trouble?" Daring asked, his face grim.

"I have no reason to think so, Jim," Kuli replied. "But I'm going to contact my friend in intelligence right away." He opened his briefcase and took out a cellular phone. "Good thing I've got this with me! "He pointed to the encrypted phone on his desk. "That's the phone Mark brought me. Why not use that to call Henri in Paris?"

"I will!" Daring said, picking up the instrument.

Soon, both men were busy talking with their friends in security.

Kuli hung up first and went to his desk. Opening a drawer, he took out a Beretta automatic and an extra clip of bullets, and slipped these into his coat pocket.

Daring put down his phone. "Henri's on the way to Düsseldorf. His assistant told me that the German police had asked him to join them at once."

"Excellent!" Kuli said. "My police contact told me he's sending men here at once. And they're going to send people to watch Herr Dantzler, for his own safety." He thought a moment. "I hope they get there in time. Dantzler left his office suddenly, and they don't know where he is."

"Where are my kids?" Daring asked. His eyes showed his anxiety.

"They were last seen leaving Dantzler's office," Kuli told him. "Then the police lost sight of them. They were primarily watching Dantzler."

"When will your phones be repaired so that David can get a call through?" Daring asked.

"Pretty soon, I should think."

Kuli was wrong, however. Calls coming into his office were being intercepted, as David was about to learn.

David stood by the public phone in the narrow hall leading from the dining room of the small restaurant and tried again to reach Herr Kuli. This time a man responded. Greatly relieved, David explained that he wanted to talk with Herr Kuli at once.

"He's having trouble with his phone line," the man replied, "but we're working on it. If it's that important, I can connect you, however. Who shall I say is calling him?" David heard the man cover the receiver and speak quietly to someone beside him.

David started to give his name—then he paused. He was beginning to get a funny feeling about this. "I'd rather not say. Herr Kuli will want to speak with me right away." David was becoming convinced that something was wrong.

"I have to tell him who's calling," the man insisted. "This is an emergency situation, and I'm trying to help you." There were several clicks on the line.

David had a sudden thought: the longer he spoke on the phone, the more time that gave people with sophisticated equipment to pinpoint the location of his call! They could be on the way right now!

He hung up and hurried back to Mark and Penny. "Let's go! I'll explain outside!"

He paid for their hot chocolate, and the three walked

quickly out of the restaurant.

"We've got to get away from here!" David said hurriedly, as they turned to their right and walked rapidly along the sidewalk. "Something's wrong with Herr Kuli's phone, and a man tried to get me to give my name. If his line's been cut and his calls are being intercepted, someone could be tracking the phone I used. We've got to get out of this neighborhood at once!"

"Boy! This is getting complicated!" Mark exclaimed.

"We've got to call Karl and Willi right away!" David said. "There's nothing else we can do! We can arrange to meet them somewhere and maybe give them the diskette. They can call Herr Kuli and he can pick it up from them. No one suspects them of being connected with Herr Kuli. The skinheads are all looking for us."

"How much time do we have before those people start picking up the money in Paris and the other cities?" Mark asked.

David looked at his watch. "Less than two hours! Maybe an hour."

Penny expressed the alarm they all were feeling now. "Herr Kuli's got to get that information to the police right away! How will they arrange those arrests in Switzerland and France and Frankfurt? Gosh, it's going to be close!"

"It won't be close at all if we can't get the diskette to Herr Kuli," David said soberly. "Look!" He pointed. "There's a taxi! Let's grab it. Maybe we should go straight to Karl and Willi's house to save time!"

CHAPTER 8

"THE KIDS ARE IN DANGER!"

I've just remembered, your kids have two German friends," Herr Kuli said suddenly to Daring. "Maybe Karl and Willi know where they are." Quickly he looked into his pocket notebook, found the number, and punched the keys of his cellular phone.

Jim Daring stood anxiously beside him as Kuli broke into rapid German. The Darings spoke French, but not German, and Jim had to wait for Kuli to explain his conversation.

In a minute he put his hand over the phone and spoke to Daring. "I've got Willi. He says that your kids haven't called them yet, but they're supposed to soon. They're all going to karate class in a little while."

"How long will Karl and Willi wait for them to call?" Daring asked quickly.

Kuli spoke into the phone again, then turned back to Daring. "They'll wait as long as we ask them to. I told them that there's been some trouble."

"Ask them to wait there until our kids call or come

66

by. When they've heard from our kids, ask Willi to call us at once," Daring said. He was pacing back and forth across the room.

Kuli relayed the message to Willi, gave him the number of his cellular phone, then hung up.

"Why don't we go to Karl and Willi's house and wait there for the kids?" Daring suggested. "That way we could bring them back ourselves and know that they were safe." Jim Daring was now very concerned for the safety of Penny and Mark and David.

"Good idea!" Kuli said. "If they call me while we're on the way, they'll get this cellular phone I have with me. We'll be that much closer to picking them up." He called his secretary on the office intercom. "Tell Paul to come here at once!" He turned to Daring.

"Paul Leitmann is new here, on loan from the bank. He's been very helpful with the financial applications we have to prepare, and he helps in other ways as well. I'll ask him to man the office for me while we go for your kids."

The intercom buzzed, and he picked up the phone. "Ja? "His face clouded. "Gone? Where has he gone? I'm expecting him to work with me all day!" He spoke a moment longer, then put down the phone. Turning to Jim Daring, he expressed complete bafflement. "Paul's gone, she says! This is most unusual. I didn't authorize him to leave, but she says he told her that I did." He pondered a moment. "I don't like this at all, Jim! Let's go to Karl and Willi's house and wait for your kids."

Hurrying from the building, Kuli and Daring got into the car and drove rapidly away.

At Karl and Willi's apartment, Mark, Penny, and David had just arrived and had begun to tell their mysterious story to the German boys. Suddenly the doorbell rang!

Karl went to the door and opened it. Paul Leitmann stood there, smiling pleasantly. "May I come in?" he asked.

When Paul entered the room, David said, "Oh, Hi, Paul."

Reassured by the fact that David knew the stranger, Karl let him in. David introduced him to the German youths, telling them that Paul worked for Herr Kuli, and was a friend.

Paul seemed very nervous, Penny noted. He began to speak rapidly. "Mr. Daring and Herr Kuli sent me to pick you up and bring you to the office," he said. "There seems to be some trouble."

"Daddy's here!" Penny said, delight in her voice. "Gosh, I feel safer already!"

"Yes, he just came in suddenly," Paul said. "But something's wrong with our phone system at the office, and we can't call out."

"I couldn't get in to Herr Kuli, either," David told him. "Someone wanted me to identify myself, but I didn't."

"I have a car," Paul said. "Please come with me at once and I'll take you to the office. They sent me for you," he added.

Just then the phone rang. "Don't wait to answer!" Paul urged. "We must go at once!"

But Willi had already picked up the receiver. "It's for you, David," he said, holding the phone out to him. David crossed the room and took it from him. Mark followed close behind.

Paul seemed very anxious now. He turned to Penny. "Your father's firm is working on a very important project with Herr Kuli, isn't that right?" he asked Penny. "Just where is this project?" He turned toward the door, and stepped back, as if to allow space for Penny to follow him and give David privacy as he spoke on the phone.

Penny took a few steps toward the door and began to reply to the friendly man, then had a sudden sense that she shouldn't. If Paul was Herr Kuli's assistant, didn't he know already what the project was? If he didn't know, then Herr Kuli hadn't shared the information with him and that meant she shouldn't either.

"Oh, I'm not sure about all the things Dad and Herr Kuli are doing," she said evasively.

"But they are working on an ancient tomb in Egypt, aren't they?" he insisted. He took another step toward the door. Penny noted that he glanced at David also. *Was he trying to hear what David was saying? Why was he so close to the door?* "Well, Dad doesn't really tell everything he's doing," she replied.

Penny's parents had warned her not to discuss the

family business in front of other people. "But what if someone asks me a direct question, and I know the answer?" she had asked. "Shouldn't I tell them? I can't tell a lie."

"You don't have to tell everything you know to people who don't need to know it," her father had told her often. "And if telling what you know might cause harm or danger to someone, you might have to say that you are unable to answer the question."

Penny remembered her father's advice, and determined not to give Paul any of the information he was seeking. Anxiously she glanced over at David, just in time to hear him tell Herr Kuli, "Don't worry, sir. We'll be very careful." Then David called to Paul, "Paul, Herr Kuli wants to talk with you."

Paul seemed shocked. He hadn't heard David whisper to Herr Kuli that he'd just arrived and had tried to get them into his car. Visibly shaken, he hesitated, as if uncertain what to do; then, reluctantly, Paul walked over to David and took the phone from his hand.

Mark and David then walked over to join Penny. Karl and Willi came close. Turning to her brother, Penny spoke very quietly in Swahili, the language they spoke in Africa. "Mark, he's been trying to pump information from me about Dad's work. I don't trust him."

David and the two German boys looked at her in surprise. They hadn't understood a word she'd said, of course.

"Neither does Herr Kuli," Mark replied, also in

Swahili. "He and Dad are on the way here to pick us up. But when I said that Paul was here, Herr Kuli told me that we should get away in a hurry. He's telling Paul to return at once. When Paul leaves, we're to give the diskette to Karl and Willi and leave. Karl and Willi are to wait for Herr Kuli and Dad to arrive. They think this place may be under observation, and they don't want us caught here, but they think Karl and Willi should be safe enough once we leave."

Just then Paul put down the phone. He looked very nervous. "I've got to do another errand for Herr Kuli," he said angrily. He rushed out the door and ran down the steps to his car.

"Quick!" Mark said, reaching into his pocket and handing the package to Karl. "This is vital information. Wait here for Herr Kuli and my dad. Don't let anyone else in. Call the police if anyone tries to break in. We've got to leave and lead suspicion away from this apartment!"

With a few more words, David clarified the situation. "We'll hurry a few blocks away, then call and tell you where we are. Herr Kuli will have the police here very quickly. Then he'll come pick us up. We'll be safer on the street, they think, with people all around us, and you boys will be safe here, once we're gone."

CHAPTER 9

"THERE THEY ARE!"

There they are!" David said suddenly, as he, Penny, and Mark left the apartment building and stood on the street. "Don't look!"

Mark and Penny stood casually beside him while David glanced past them and described the car.

"The skinheads," David explained. "They're in a green Volvo at the corner. Gosh, the car's packed with men!"

"What are they doing?" Penny asked, looking deliberately in the other direction from the car David had seen.

David turned his head away from the Volvo and pointed across the street, as if discussing the building opposite. "Just waiting. And looking. Looking this way, in fact." His face was grim.

"Let's go the other way, then," Mark said, "and hope they follow us. We've got to draw them away from Karl and Willi."

They turned to their right and walked briskly along

the sidewalk, looking around as they did so, pretending to be tourists interested in everything they saw. "I feel eyes boring into my back!" Penny said.

"So do I," Mark agreed. "Let's hope they follow us. We're safe with people on the street like this. But it sure is nerve-wracking."

"Except that we'd be easy targets if they stopped at the curb and jumped us," David observed. "Maybe we better duck down one of these pedestrian alleys between the buildings. The Volvo can't follow us there!"

"Right!" Mark agreed. "Great idea! What about this one?"

"Let's go!" David said.

They dashed between the buildings, glancing behind them as they did so. The Volvo had drawn close! Then they were racing along a narrow passage, a pedestrian walkway with only a few people strolling along it.

Suddenly, they heard yells behind them! "They're after us, all right!" Mark said as he led the way. "Let's shake 'em!"

They raced down the alley and through to the other side of the block. Looking back, they saw four skinheads sprinting down the alley toward them.

"Look!" Penny said, pointing to the right. "There's another alley in the block across the street.

They dashed across the street, raced past several buildings, then ducked into the narrow walkway. Two old men were walking toward them. Otherwise the alley was deserted. David looked back just as they entered the narrow passage.

"They saw us!" he said. "Keep running!"

Mark led the way, running smoothly. Penny was right behind him, and David behind her.

"That Volvo won't have any idea where we've gone," David said. "We've just got to shake the men behind us and we'll be free!"

They rushed out onto the sidewalk at the other end of the block, dodged surprised pedestrians, almost ran into a crowd of Japanese tourists, and then turned right.

"We're getting a good lead," David said, glancing over his shoulder. "I think those guys are still in the alley. Let's duck in here before they reach the street and see us!"

They dodged quickly down another narrow passage and sprinted past a couple of people. David looked back just as they entered the alley. None of the pursuers was visible!

"They're still in that other block," he said, "and they didn't see us!"

"Thank the Lord!" Penny said gratefully.

They came to the other end of the block, slowed down as they emerged onto the sidewalk, and looked both ways. They were on a wide boulevard.

"There's a street car!" Mark said.

"Grab it!" David replied. The three dashed into the street to the platform and jammed themselves through the tram's door just before it closed. David led Mark and Penny to the back.

They sat down, breathing deeply from the run, and looked anxiously through the window of the moving car to see if their pursuers were in sight.

"I don't see them," Penny whispered.

"Neither do I!" David said as he turned from the window.

They began to relax. "At least we led them away from Karl and Willi's," David said gratefully. "I saw only one car and it's been chasing us, so the boys and the diskette should be safe. Your dad and Herr Kuli should have picked them up by now."

"We got away just in time!" Mark added.

"Well, it's a good thing those guys had only one car," David said. "They had to follow us. That left the coast clear for the others. Gosh," he said, changing the subject, "I hope they get the diskette printed out in time to call the police in those other cities."

"So do I," Mark agreed. "You know, Penny, if you hadn't been suspicious of Paul, or if Dad hadn't warned me with that call, we'd be their prisoners by now."

"Yeah," David said, "and maybe we'd all be in a garage full of skinheads! That was close!"

"Now that we got away, we've got to call Herr Kuli and Dad," Penny reminded them.

"But let's watch for that Volvo," Mark warned. "We don't want them to spot us in this streetcar—we'd be trapped for sure."

David had been looking out the window. "I think we're heading back downtown!" he said suddenly.

"We'll be able to find a phone."

A few blocks later, David looked out the window and was surprised to recognize their location. "That's Herr Dantzler's bank ahead!" he said.

Penny looked where he pointed. "Hey, is that Herr Dantzler on the sidewalk?"

"It is!" David agreed. "That's him. Wonder where he's headed?" He thought a second. "Should we get off and join him? He could tell us where to find a phone."

"I don't know," Mark answered thoughtfully. "He might have people following him."

"But he knows where he's going, and he could probably help us call your dad. They're waiting to pick us up before going back to Herr Kuli's office to print out the diskette and call the police."

"You're right, David." Mark said. "Let's get off at the next stop and join him."

The streetcar passed Herr Dantzler by half a block before stopping. Looking carefully in all directions, the three Americans got off and began to walk back along the sidewalk toward Herr Dantzler. The banker was striding briskly in their direction.

Penny suddenly grabbed Mark's arm. "Is that Mercedes following Herr Dantzler!" she said, alarm in her voice.

Startled, Mark and David saw a black Mercedes heading toward them, moving slowly along the curb, drawing close behind Herr Dantzler. Obviously, he hadn't seen it.

"Could be we've gotten ourselves in the middle again!" Mark said.

"What's that inside the car?" David asked suddenly, as they came close to the banker and the Mercedes behind him.

Just then Dantzler recognized them and waved.

"Down, Herr Dantzler!" David yelled suddenly, pointing to the car that had come swiftly beside Dantzler. "Duck!"

Dantzler stopped, startled. He looked toward the curb and saw the Mercedes, then threw himself suddenly forward to the ground.

An arrow flashed from the back seat of the Mercedes and buried itself in the brick building.

At once the Mercedes increased speed and pulled away from the curb. Behind the tinted glass, the Americans saw angry faces staring at them as the vehicle sped past.

"David, that's Hoffmann!" Penny said in shocked surprise.

"Hoffmann! Here?" David answered.

"How'd you spot that crossbow?" Mark asked David, as they ran to help Herr Dantzler to his feet.

"It was just sticking out the back window of the car," David replied.

Dantzler jumped up as they reached him.

"Thanks, David! Follow me!" he said, leading them suddenly into the entrance of the store beside them. "This way!"

The three rushed after the banker, through the front door of an elegant clothing store, all the way to the back of the building. Clearly, Dantzler knew the place.

"Through here!" he said, opening a narrow door and ignoring the brass letters that said "PRIVATE." They hurried after him, and David closed the door when they were through. Dantzler led them quickly along a narrow and dark, paneled passageway.

He stopped suddenly, took some keys out of his pocket, and unlocked a door to his right. He went in and they followed, wondering where they were and where the banker was leading them.

They found themselves in a small office. Dantzler turned and faced them. His face was grim.

"Thanks! Your warning saved my life! That man shot at me with a crossbow."

"Who was it?" Mark asked.

"His name is Fritz Heller," Dantzler answered. "He's a banker. He's also a sportsman. And he's a dedicated Communist. Others worked for the KGB and the STASI for the power and the privileges. He serves them because he believes in the Marxist cause. The men blackmailing me said he would help me escape from the police after I wired the money to the banks."

"It was a trap, wasn't it?" David asked.

"That's right, David," Dantzler agreed. "It was a trap. Just this morning Fritz was in my office, giving me directions for my escape."

"Then why did he try to kill you, Herr Dantzler?"

Penny asked.

"Because I didn't wait for him to come pick me up," Dantzler answered. "That was the plan. But I knew it was a trap. They were watching for me, and when I left before I was supposed to, they knew I was getting away. They know also that I can identify them to the police."

"How'd you know when to leave?" Mark asked.

"I just had a sudden conviction that I should get out while I was still alone. So I told the secretary I'd be right back, headed for the men's room in the back of our office space, and went out the side door!"

"What'll we do now?" David asked anxiously.

"I'll call Kuli and tell him what's happened. Then we'll get out of this building. The STASI will pinpoint this place as soon as my call gets into Herr Kuli's office."

"You can't call in to Herr Kuli's office, Herr Dantzler," Mark said. "They've got the phones tapped. He and my dad are waiting for us to call so they can pick us up, but we can't get through to them!"

"Herr Kuli has a mobile phone, though," Dantzler told them, reaching into his pocket for his address book. He opened the pages, then picked up the phone from the desk and dialed. As he waited for Kuli to answer, he glanced over at Mark. "Where's that package with the diskette?"

"We gave it to two German friends. They're at their apartment now, waiting for Herr Kuli and Dad to pick them up."

Just then Dantzler heard Kuli answer the phone. Quickly he told of the attack on his life and of running into the three teenagers. "I know how to get away from here," he told Kuli. "Why don't I lead these three to safety, then call you when we're clear?" He listened to Kuli's reply. "All right," he agreed.

Suddenly he frowned at the phone, then looked over at the teenagers. "We've been jammed." He put down the receiver. "Someone jammed the phone! But Kuli said they can't wait any longer. They've got to print out that diskette and get the information to the police. I can get us away quicker than they could come get us anyway. We'll get out of this neighborhood, then join them. By that time, they'll have police protecting their office."

He frowned. "Kuli will not have much time to make those calls! The police will need time to make arrangements for arresting the men who are going to the banks to get the money. They've got to reach police in Frankfurt, Bern, and Paris. This could be terrible if they can't catch those men when they come to the banks!" His face showed great anxiety.

"How much money did you wire to those banks, sir?" Mark asked.

"Six million deutsche marks!" Dantzler replied, his face pale.

"Gosh!" Mark exclaimed, awed at the amount.

"But we must get away from here at once!" Dantzler said decisively. "Follow me!"

Feet pounded suddenly down a hall behind the door

to their left. Someone turned the handle, found that it was locked, then shook it violently.

CHAPTER 10

RACE TO THE RHINE!

Dantzler's face went white. He waved the teenagers to the door through which they'd come. "Quick!" he whispered.

But, David thought, as they rushed back into the hallway, *what if men were blocking that exit also?*

But there was no one in sight. Dantzler turned right, away from the store entrance through which they'd entered the hall. "This way!" he said urgently, locking the door and hurrying after them. They rushed down the narrow, paneled hall. It ended abruptly before another locked door.

Quickly Dantzler unlocked the door and let them through. Here they found themselves in a small room, bare of furniture, with another door opposite them. The banker led them to this door, unlocked it, and let them out into the street. Locking this door behind him, with his eyes he searched the sidewalk to each side. Pedestrians passed from both directions and cars filled the street before them.

"Do you see any of the men who chased you?" Dantzler asked them, as they stood wondering which way to go.

"No, sir," Mark answered. David agreed.

"Let's go this way, then," Dantzler said, turning left and leading them at a fast pace along the sidewalk. They wove their way through the pedestrians as they hurried toward the corner. "If you see a taxi, signal it," he told them.

Nervously scanning the faces they passed and the cars that passed quickly along the street, Dantzler and the three Americans arrived at the corner. Still, they'd not seen anyone suspicious.

"Cross the street!" Dantzler commanded quietly. "Those men will come out that same door we did in a minute. We've got to be out of sight behind these crowds."

They crossed with a crowd of people when the light changed and continued along the sidewalk of the next block. Frantically now, they searched the street for empty taxis, but found none.

"Quick!" Dantzler said suddenly. "We'll get that tram!" He darted through traffic and the three followed him to the streetcar platform and the waiting tram. They hurried on board, paid, and moved to the back.

"How did you have keys to the building we went into, Herr Dantzler?" Penny asked wonderingly.

"That department store is one of our bank's best customers, Penny," he replied. "They let me have a private office there. It's been useful before, but never so useful as today!"

"Where are we going now, sir?" David asked as the streetcar picked up speed and left the downtown area.

"To the Rhine River," the banker replied. His eyes searched the other passengers of the streetcar continually, as well as the cars that they passed on the street. "I have a boat there. We'll take that, go up the river, then land and take a cab."

In the back seat of the black Mercedes a half block behind the streetcar, Hoffmann took a portable phone from his briefcase. He punched a series of numbers, then spoke quietly into the machine, giving crisp orders. Back in the heart of the business district, the green Volvo turned a corner, went around the block, and headed toward the river.

Turning to Fritz Heller, Hoffmann smiled. "We've got them now. This streetcar goes toward the Rhine. I think Dantzler's headed for the river. We'll get him before he leaves the shore!"

Fritz Heller was grim. "If those kids hadn't warned him, I'd have pinned Dantzler against the wall with the arrow!" He was shaking with anger.

"You'll get him at the river," Hoffmann assured him. "We can't use guns because they'd be heard. Your crossbow is silent. You'll get him."

"We'll have to get those kids, too," the stocky man beside the driver said quietly. "They can identify us,

I think."

"Yes, we'll have to get them, too," Hoffmann agreed. He was violently angry. Then he controlled his rage at their failure to shoot Dantzler with the satisfying thought that he'd finally have his revenge on those American teenagers who'd ruined every one of his projects this summer.

Back at Kuli's office, the atmosphere was tense. With quiet efficiency Kuli had inserted the diskette into his private computer and brought up the document it contained. He switched on the printer. Then he looked at his watch.

"We have so little time!" he said bitterly.

"It's printing now," Jim Daring said.

"But will we get this information to the police in time?" Kuli asked. He sat before the printer, reading as the words were printed. Ripping off the first page, he grabbed his mobile phone. Quickly he reached the police officer who'd been assigned to this case. He read the name of the bank in Frankfurt, the number of the transaction Herr Dantzler had wired there, the account number to which the money had been sent, and the name and description of the man who would pick up the money: all this was included in the information Herr Dantzler had put on the diskette.

The printer continued to print out information while Kuli spoke on the phone. When he finished, Daring ripped off the next page with information concerning the banks in Basel and Paris. Kuli read this also. The policeman took notes even as his tape machine recorded all the information Kuli gave him.

Kuli listened for the response. "All right," he agreed. He continued to read off the printed pages, while the recorder in the police office continued to take the vital information. Three pages later, Kuli finished. He put down the phone.

"They're calling the special police in all those cities, Jim," he said, smiling. "They have all the information Dantzler collected on the KGB and the STASI: names of secret agents in business, the universities and schools, government, and, of course, the media and the arts. This is an incredible haul!"

"What about my kids?" Jim Daring asked tensely. He'd become more and more worried about them.

"Dantzler will bring them here shortly. He was confident he could get away." Kuli leaned back in his chair and relaxed for the first time in an hour. "It looks like those teenagers of yours have helped foil an incredible theft that would have given six million deutsche marks to the Communist secret police! They helped Dantzler escape. He said they saved his life! You've got to be proud of them!"

"I certainly am!" Jim Daring agreed. "But I won't be happy until I see them."

"Neither will I, Jim," Kuli agreed. "Neither will I. We should see them in half an hour." They've got to be relaxing now, happy in what they've accomplished."

CHAPTER 11

"THOSE BOATS ARE CATCHING UP!"

On the streetcar nearing the river, the three teenagers were indeed relaxing. Penny and David sat together; Mark and Dantzler sat across from them. They talked quietly among themselves, thankful now that the danger was now past. Dantzler smiled pleasantly as they spoke, but his eyes never ceased searching the cars that passed them when the streetcar stopped to discharge and take on passengers.

Finally he rose. "This is it," he said. "We get off here."

The car stopped. Dantzler led the way, looking quickly around as he stepped to the platform. He saw nothing suspicious. "It looks as if we're clear," he smiled. "Let's go."

He led them to the corner, then across the street. They hurried along a narrow lane with houses on each side, each with window boxes of flowers.

"Oh, this is lovely!" Penny exclaimed, stopping. "Can we look a minute, Herr Dantzler?" she asked, her eyes shining at a quaint old gray house decked with red flower boxes outside its dormer windows.

"Not just yet, Penny," Dantzler smiled. "Let's get back to Herr Kuli's office first. Then, when everything's settled, I promise I'll bring you back. You can take all the pictures you want. In fact, I'm so grateful for what you three have done for me, and for Germany, that I'll give you all the film you can use!"

They laughed and continued their rapid pace to the river. When they reached the water, Dantzler led them to a long dock where small motorboats and sailboats were tied up. Expensive-looking powerboats lined each side of the dock. Dantzler went halfway to the end, and stopped at a sleek craft painted dark blue, with windows in the bow, indicating a room below deck, and a high glass-enclosed cabin with a white roof.

"Here we are," he said gratefully. "Get in and we'll take a cruise. I'm finally beginning to relax a little!" He laughed as they climbed into the boat. "David, toss off that bow line, will you? And Mark, do the same at the stern. Penny, if you'll take this key and go below you'll find some life jackets for us in the lockers under the bunks."

Penny unlocked the narrow door and went down the steps to the sleeping area below. Dantzler took the seat behind the wheel, inserted the key, and started the engine. When the boys threw off the lines the banker wasted no time. He steered the boat away from the dock, turned, and shook off his jacket as he headed into the river.

"Now we're safe! At last!" He laughed happily.

The glass windshield shattered before his face as the arrow struck and went through, sending pieces flying all over the bow of the boat. Half the windshield was gone.

"Down!" Dantzler called as he shoved the throttle and jerked the wheel violently to the left. The boat leaped ahead, swerved, and raced out into the fast-moving river.

Thrown to the deck by the sudden turn, Mark and David looked up in astonishment. Penny climbed up the steps from the cabin below. She'd been thrown onto one of the bunks.

"What happened?" she cried.

They all saw the broken glass strewn all about the deck.

"Hold on!" Dantzler shouted as he swerved the boat violently to the right. He looked back to the dock, and the three teenagers did, too.

To their horror they saw that a black Mercedes had driven right to the edge of the boat landing. A green Volvo was just pulling up and men were tumbling out and racing along the dock. Some were already piling into a large black powerboat. At the very end of the dock, still quite close to Dantzler's boat, Fritz knelt and frantically reloaded his crossbow.

"Hoffmann's gang followed us!" Dantzler said

bleakly. "Hold on! We've got to get away!"

Back on the dock, a blond man ran up behind the man with the crossbow, and the kids recognized him at once.

"That's Hoffmann!" Penny cried in alarm.

Dantzler pushed the throttle to the limit and swerved again to foil Fritz's aim. The arrow flashed from the dock, passed to the side of the boat, and skipped a half a dozen times on the river before it sank.

"Put on those lifejackets!" Dantzler called.

The current was rapid and the wind strong on their faces as the three teenagers stared anxiously ahead, then turned back toward the landing. A large, black powerboat was pulling out at great speed, the high white wake curving behind each side of the rising bow as the craft headed directly toward them like an arrow shot from a bow. Taking the binoculars Dantzler handed him, David focused on their pursuers.

"That's Hoffmann, all right!" he said. "And the *Crossbowman's* beside him!"

Just then Dantzler spun the wheel again, and the speeding craft swerved sharply to the right, then resumed course as it passed a long, low barge pushed by a white, steel tug. Two more tugs of the same kind and color were in line ahead of this one, and they soon had passed them all.

Penny sat down next to Herr Dantzler, while Mark and David went to the back of the boat. Looking anxiously behind, Penny saw the speedboat in the distance, high white wakes curving away from its bow on both sides.

"That black boat's fast, Herr Dantzler," Penny said.

"I know it is, Penny," Dantzler said, his face grim. "I'm hoping we can just get to a landing up river before they catch us."

"There's another boat right behind the black one!" Mark called out suddenly.

David focused the binoculars on the second boat that raced toward them and was shocked at what he saw. He yelled out above the noise of the boat's engine, "It's filled with skinheads!".

Dantzler's expression grew even more bleak as he looked back and spotted the other boat. Then he gave his attention once more to the traffic ahead. They were fast approaching a tour boat, whose two enclosed decks were dotted with large rectangular windows. Twin stacks rose at each side of the boat's stern. A roofed cabin, open at the sides, was on top of the upper deck. Dantzler altered course and they passed this boat also.

The shore to their right was bounded by a sloping wall of gray stone. People walked along the top of the wall, enjoying the river.

"They don't seem to have a care in the world!" Mark said to David.

"They sure don't have to worry about crossbows and skinheads!" David agreed. "That arrow could have killed one of us! The boys sat down in chairs fixed to the deck and turned their eyes to the pursuing boats.

Their own craft was flying across the water at top speed, its engine making a great noise, its white wake climbing high into the air behind on both sides.

Where do you think Herr Dantzler will land so we can get off?" David asked.

"I don't know," Mark replied, "but I think those boats are catching up."

"I think they are, too!" David said. He turned and called over the noise of the engine and the wind. "Herr Dantzler, those boats are getting close!"

"I know they are, David," the banker replied anxiously. "I'm trying to reach a landing before they do."

Penny rose and holding tightly to the boat's rail, went back to join the boys at the stern. She knelt between the two boys, gripping the backs of their deck chairs for balance. "Can we get away from those boats?" she asked. The wind blew her hair around her face.

Mark, deeply troubled, looked into her anxious eyes. "I don't see how, Penny. Look how fast they're coming!"

"But what can they do to us in broad daylight on the open river? All kinds of people can see us!" she said.

"Well, that didn't stop them from shooting an arrow at Herr Dantzler in front of the department store!" Mark reminded her.

"And they shot at us as we left the dock," David added. Suddenly David got up. "I'll ask Herr Dantzler if he's got any weapons on board. There's got to be *something* we can do to defend ourselves!"

"Ask if he's got any flares!" Mark said quickly. "We all know how to handle those! We can use them to signal for help."

Leaning forward to keep his balance on the steeply sloping deck, David crossed to Herr Dantzler's chair. Penny turned and watched him talk with Herr Dantzler, while Mark stared at the pursuing speedboats. They were closer.

Penny saw Dantzler shake his head and her heart sank. "Oh, Mark, he's shaking his head! I don't think he's got anything on board!"

"But he's got to have flares!" Mark insisted, getting up and heading toward Dantzler and David. "Let's ask if we can search the room below for some."

Penny followed her brother to the enclosed cabin. The wind roared through the broken glass on the left side, but the windshield was still whole on Dantzler's side.

"Go ahead and look," Dantzler said desperately. "But I don't know that we have anything to fight those men off. I used to have a flare pistol on the boat somewhere. This is a pleasure boat. I never thought I'd be attacked on the Rhine!"

David plunged down the four steps and into the enclosed cabin below. Mark and Penny followed. They threw open drawers and closet doors, above the bunks, below them, searching in every nook and cranny for anything that would help them defend themselves from their determined pursuers.

The two boats behind came closer and closer with terrifying aim.

Dantzler's face was desolate—there was no boat landing in view!

CHAPTER 12

TRANQUILLITY TOURS AND THE BASEL ZOO

Almost a mile ahead of them, trouble was brewing. The *Rhine Rose*, a flat cargo boat with a high bridge at the stern, smelled like anything but a rose as it bounced in the choppy and rapidly flowing river. The nasty smell came from the animals on board, and the crew was sick of it.

Stacked all about the deck in cages was a menagerie of animals. There were cages of monkeys chattering away, tall giraffes waved their heads on tall necks above the boat, and in cages that had tops, but no sides, were four hippos.

The giant beasts weighed more than the *Rhine Rose's* captain liked to think about. The captain thought he'd made a good deal on this contract to take the animals from a zoo in Basel, Switzerland, to one in northern Germany. But now, Captain Zeller wasn't so sure.

The four giraffes were no trouble. They just smelled bad. Their tall necks stretching out and up and drew the attention of people on shore as well as that of passengers in the boats they passed. The two dozen monkeys were noisy, but posed no threat to the boat at all. They could get as mad as they wished, they still weren't able to break out of their cages.

But the hippos were another matter. They were mad not only because the uneven motion of the boat kept them struggling for balance, they were also mad because the cold wind coming in through the sides of their cages was striking their tropical skins. And, they were also mad because they were hungry. Their keepers, fearful of the consequences, hadn't dared feed them for some time.

A dozen times that day the foreman in charge of the animals had stormed up to the bridge of the tug demanding that the captain slow the boat and quit annoying the hippos by blowing his whistle and sounding the boat's horn.

"I'm warning you, Zeller," the stout man shouted from the tug's open port into the cabin, "if you push these beasts too far they'll break the cages and tear your boat apart! Slow down—or stop the rocking! And stop those whistles and horns!"

"And I tell *you*, sir," the captain replied in a fury, "that there are rules for boats on this river! I *can't* slow down. And I didn't make the river current. Blame God! And I have to signal with the horn and the whistle. I told you all this before you signed the contract! You agreed that your animals could take it. Now, make them take it!"

The foreman shook his head and shouted back. In a cold rage, Captain Zeller turned to his bosun's mate: "Throw him out!"

The big bosun advanced toward the smaller man, who fled at once, slamming the port. Cursing wildly, the foreman climbed down the ladder to the deck and stormed toward the bow. Moving forward, he stopped behind the hippos' cages. The giant animals had already bent some of the bars in their cage with their angry shoving.

Back in the bridge of the big tug, Captain Zeller had other things on his mind. They were about to overtake the weirdest tour boat he'd ever seen and he had to give his full attention to passing the vessel safely. He stared at the strange boat.

It was long and flat, with two decks. It's open upper deck was lined with people in wheelchairs on both sides of the boat. The craft was wider than an ordinary tour boat, and on the rear deck a strange contraption soared some forty feet toward the sky, leaning at a strange angle. The Captain thought that it looked like a model of the Leaning Tower of Pisa, but it couldn't be, could it? It could be, and it was. The model was being transported at great expense to satisfy the whim of Archibald Alexander Armstrong, the multimillionaire passenger in the wheelchair nearest the stern. He had taken a fancy to it when the tour group had visited the famous tower in the city of Pisa, Italy, and he'd insisted on buying the model on the spot.

Tranquillity Tours boasted that its customers were the happiest travelers in the world of international touring. An amazing claim to make, especially when you realized that the tour company catered not to the young, the nimble, and the fit, but to well-heeled, senior citizens in wheel-chairs. Folks who'd lost the ability to move themselves around easily. Folks who wouldn't otherwise have thought that they could ever take tours and cruises ever again.

But Tranquillity Tours of Topeka, Kansas, existed just to disprove such negative thoughts. The brainchild of Sylvester Carpeggio, Tranquillity Tours had proved for the past seventeen years that being in a wheelchair was no reason not to see the world. You didn't to be able to walk, you just needed money. That's all. Just money. And money was what these passengers had.

Sylvester Carpeggio had made his millions in his career as a hotel proprietor. Now he wanted to take the old, the less able, the immobile on tours of Europe, and so he'd used his money to construct tour buses the likes of which the touring world had never seen. They were equipped with several elevators to lift the passengers smoothly from the pavement to the bus floor. They had comfortable lounge chairs, sofas, beds, and baths. They possessed well-stocked refreshment refrigerators and efficient kitchens. Above all, the passengers were cared for and coddled by an incredibly well-trained staff.

This tour had picked up its passengers in Topeka and flown them to Hamburg, Germany. After two days of rest and recuperation in a chartered hotel, the refreshed tour group set off to see the sights. It was in Italy that Mr. Archibald Alexander Armstrong had fallen in love with the model of the Leaning Tower of Pisa.

"I've *got* to have it!" he'd insisted to Luis Carpeggio, the son of Sylvester, who was in charge of this particular tour. "I don't care what it costs."

"You *shall* have it, Mr. Armstrong," Luis said smoothly.

But Tony, the assistant director of the tour, was flabbergasted at this.

"How in the world will we get that contraption across the mountains?"

"We'll *find* a way, Tony."

"But it won't go on our buses!" Tony insisted. His long, thin, black mustache quivered anxiously as he rolled his dark eyes at the impossible task.

"Then buy a truck with a flatbed trailer and let that follow our buses back to the Rhine," Luis Carpeggio said. "In Hamburg, rent a transport plane and stick the tower in it. *That's* how we'll get it back to the States!"

"Buy a truck and trailer? Rent a cargo plane to cross the Atlantic! That will cost a *fortune*!" Tony quivered.

"Mr. Armstrong has a fortune, Tony," Luis replied

firmly. "And Tranquillity Tours *always* finds a way. What our customers want, and can pay for, they get! Take care of it, Tony."

And that was that. The specially designed and equipped, exceedingly stable and smooth-riding boat was returning the happy tour group to Rotterdam. The remarkable stabilizing fins on the hull made the voyage as smooth as if they'd been on a millpond in the middle of Kansas. The breeze on the river was strong, but the rails of the second deck were lined with people in wheelchairs and lounge chairs, eager voyagers, inquisitively scanning the banks of the river and the boats they passed.

The strange-looking leaning tower perched precariously on the rear deck of the boat attracted the surprised stares of *everyone* on the river. Mr. Archibald Alexander Armstrong was craning his neck to study his tower looming up at a strange angle from the stern. Had it swayed?

On the bridge of the cargo boat fast overtaking Tranquillity Tours, Captain Zeller put the hippos out of his mind as he gave his attention to passing the vessel ahead. Quietly, he issued his orders. The man at the wheel changed course slightly and the heavily-laden cargo vessel edged to the left and began to pass the tour boat.

Already, some of the passengers of Tranquillity Tours had spotted the long necks and small heads of the giraffes towering above the approaching craft. A crowd of wheelchairs began to cluster at the stern of the upper deck of the tour boat.

Looking back from the bridge of the Tranquillity Tours tour boat, Captain Hamm was attentive, but not worried, as he watched the cargo boat approach and prepare to pass. He spoke to his helmsman, and the tour boat edged a bit to the right, toward the bank but with a comfortable distance between ship and shore.

"Let's give him all the space he needs," Captain Hamm said with a smile. "The fins on our hull will keep the passengers from feeling the slightest jar from that boat's wake."

Nothing could be simpler than the maneuver the cargo boat was about to execute. Nothing could interfere with the smooth professionalism of the tour boat's crew and the manner in which they kept even the busy Rhine traffic from causing their passengers the slightest inconvenience.

"Our Customers—The Happiest Travelers in the World of Touring," the sign on the boat proclaimed. The ship's crew was proud of that sign. Those happy travelers were about to get the biggest surprise of their lives.

CHAPTER 13

"WE'RE GOING TO HIT THAT BOAT!"

The tension on the boat in which Dantzler and the three American teenagers were fleeing for their lives had become unbearable. Behind them, Hoffmann's two boats were quickly approaching the range where Fritz could begin to fire his crossbow. While Dantzler steered the racing craft, Mark, Penny, and David searched the cabin frantically for flares or weapons or anything they could use to defend themselves from their pursuers. They found maps, ropes, and tools of all kinds—but no weapon.

Then Mark gave a sudden shout. "Here's a flare gun!" and he held up a long, ungainly signal pistol. "Now, if we can just find some shells for it."

"What does that thing do?" Penny asked, grabbing for the wall as the boat veered suddenly and threw them all off balance.

"It fires a flare high in the air. Anywhere in the

world it's a signal asking for help . All we need is some shells to go in it. They're like shotgun shells, only longer and thicker! There's *got* to be some somewhere!"

"You two keep looking!" David said as he rushed up the steps to join Dantzler.

"They're close, David!" Dantzler said, desperation in his voice. "Watch them while I dodge these boats ahead!"

Dantzler swerved and roared past a long barge being pushed by a tall gray tug. They bounced wildly as the wake from the speedboat hit them. Looking behind, David saw that the black boat pursuing them was less than forty yards away. Its companion, a red craft, had drawn even with it. Then both boats swerved suddenly and passed on the far side of the tug and barge. They were temporarily lost from view. In a moment both reappeared as they passed the barge even closer now. "Look! There's the *Crossbowman*!" David said suddenly. "I saw his bow for a second and then he lowered it. Do you think he'd dare to shoot us in plain sight like this?"

"All he has to do is hit the person steering, David. Tell me when to duck!" Dantzler said.

"He's about to shoot!" David said suddenly. "Duck!"

They both fell to the deck. Another piece of the windshield shattered before them. Dantzler jumped back to the seat to guide the craft.

"He'll have to take a minute to reload!" David said.

David was wrong. Seconds later the *Crossbowman* was aiming again. Two men knelt beside him, one on either side, their bodies shielding his crossbow from viewers on the river and the bank.

"He's shooting again!" David said as he dropped again to the deck. Dantzler was beside him.

This time the arrow slammed into the instrument panel between the rim and the hub of the wheel—in exactly the same spot where Dantzler had been sitting a moment before!

Just then Mark and Penny rushed up from the lower cabin. "Penny found some shells for the signal pistol!" Mark exclaimed.

"You'd better fire at Hoffmann's boat right now!" David told Mark.

Mark and David rushed to the stern. David saw the *Crossbowman* aiming at them again. "Watch out! He's shooting again!"

Dantzler looked back frantically—and saw to his horror that Penny was standing up, looking at the pursuing boats. Leaving his seat he grabbed her shoulders, shoved her to the deck, and then turned back to grab the wheel.

The arrow flashed toward the banker and struck him in the back, near his right shoulder. Dantzler fell to his knees.

Hoffmann yelled triumphantly, "You got him, Fritz! You got him!"

The skinheads in the red boat beside Hoffmann's craft cheered as they saw the banker fall.

"Shoot all of them, Fritz," Hoffmann commanded grimly. "We can't let any of them escape." Now, at last, he was getting his revenge on those American teenagers!

And at this very moment his men would be picking up six million Deutsche marks from all those different banks. The entire plan was being crowned with glorious success! He had won!

On Dantzler's boat, Penny leaped up with a cry and rushed to the stricken man. Dantzler, still kneeling, gripped the back of the chair with one hand. The arrow had pierced his life jacket and was half-buried in his shoulder.

His driverless boat raced toward the gap between the boat carrying the animals and Tranquillity Tours' boat.

David rushed forward and grabbed the wheel. Looking back at the pursuing boats, he yelled desperately to his companions, "Hold on! I'm going to try something."

He shoved the throttle almost closed. The boat slowed at once! Then David whipped the wheel sharply to the left, turning directly toward Hoffmann's craft bearing down on them!

The wake of Dantzler's craft washed across the rapidly decreasing space between the two boats and slammed into the black boat, knocking down Fritz and the two men who shielded him. Yelling with fright,

Hoffmann's man turned the wheel to his left to avoid
Dantzler's boat, which suddenly had appeared in front
of him. He turned directly toward the red boat carrying
the skinheads. It was just a few yards away!

The bright flash from the flare gun in Mark's hand
shot toward the black boat. Screaming with terror the
men on board ducked wildly and the flare roared over
their heads. Hoffmann stumbled forward as the boat
made its sharp turn. He fell and smashed his nose on
the deck.

The red boat swerved violently to the left, barely
avoiding a crash with Hoffmann's craft. Then, both
boats hit the wake of Dantzler's boat and bounced
wildly as they raced through the rough water—straight
toward a huge barge coming toward them!

Back on Dantzler's boat, David shoved the throttle
to top speed and, swerving back to the right, roared
through the very narrow channel between the *Rhine
Rose* with its animals and Tranquillity Tours' boat. A
huge wake of cold river water climbed high on both
sides and behind Dantzler's boat. Then, it came crash-
ing down on the animals' boat!

Everything seemed to happen at once!

The sudden flood of water from the wake of
Dantzler's boat soaked the senior citizens in their rows
of wheelchairs on Tranquillity Tours' upper deck.
Hearing their cries, Luis Carpeggio turned just in time
to see his precious passengers get drenched. He cried
out in shock at this catastrophic insult to his cargo of

pampered passengers.

Captain Hamm, on Tranquillity Tours' bridge, saw Dantzler's boat race past and swerve to the right just ahead of him. He shouted to his helmsman to turn and avoid the speeding craft. Tranquillity Tours began to turn directly toward the *Rhine Rose* with its load of animals from the Basel zoo.

In trying to avoid the barge coming at them, both of the motor boats had now turned violently to their right. All eyes on board continued to stare at the vessel that had loomed so close to the, so no one saw that they were now racing directly toward Captain Zeller's *Rhine Rose* with its load of animals.

Captain Zeller heard his crewman shout at the speedboats approaching so recklessly and, turning to see what the problem might be, his shocked eyes saw the two craft aimed directly at his ship! Not wasting a moment to give orders to the helmsman, he grabbed the wheel himself and jerked it violently. Right toward Tranquillity Tours!

The wave from Dantzler's passing boat had not only drenched the shocked senior citizens to the right, but also the animals on Zeller's boat to the left. The monkeys in their cages went wild as the cold water washed over them. The giraffes waved their long necks in shocked outrage at the sudden deluge. And the hippos . . . the hippos went berserk! With mighty bellowing, they charged the bars of their cages in violent rage.

"Jump!" Hoffmann screamed frantically as his motorboat, now out of control, shot toward the cargo of animals. He and his men leaped off both sides of the boat just before it crashed into the *Rhine Rose's* steel side and blew up with tremendous force.

Skinheads from the other motorboat barely jumped from their craft before it, too, blew up with a tremendous explosion.

The thunderous explosions and towering clouds of smoke ten yards from their faces was the final straw for the hippos. Driven frantic by the crash and resulting explosions, the maddened, drenched beasts went wild. Bellowing with fear and rage, they whirled and went straight out of their of their cages as if the bars had been made of paper. Dashing toward the other side of the boat, they plunged into the Rhine and started swimming toward Tranquillity Tours!

Panicked by the tilting of the boat as the hippos rushed toward one side, the animal's attendants rushed up and down the cages of the giraffes and monkeys, flipping the catches, and wrenching open the doors. They had been instructed to do this if the boat was in danger of sinking, so that the animals could swim to safety! They were sure the boat was going to sink any moment.

The minute the cages were opened, the giraffes galloped the few feet to the rail and plunged, just behind the hippos, into the Rhine. Two dozen monkeys leaped from their cages to the boat's railing, stopped, and then began to run in circles on the deck, screaming at the top of their lungs.

On the bridge of Tranquillity Tours, Captain Hamm stared in horror at the approaching cargo ship. Its turn away from Hoffmann's boats had caused it to veer directly toward his boat. Jumping in front of the helmsman, he grabbed the wheel and jerked it into a sharp right turn.

Tranquillity Tours' attendants had rushed to comfort their bedraggled charges in wheelchairs, but the feisty senior citizens fought them off and rolled their wheelchairs to the boat's railing to see what would happen to the swimming hippos and giraffes.

That earlier sharp turn to the right had been too violent for the lines securing the Leaning Tower of Pisa to the Tranquillity Tours' deck. The tower shuddered, then began to fall to the left—toward the rapidly approaching *Rhine Rose*!

Just as the hippos and giraffes swimming in the water faded from view behind the stern of the two vessels, the passengers were startled by cries from the deck crew, "We're going to hit that ship!"

Both captains saw their mortal peril at the same time and both tried with all their might to keep the vessels from colliding. They yelled for the engines to be stopped, and as the engine rooms cut all power, the two ships pulled together more slowly. Then they slowed on a parallel course—just twenty feet apart!

The Leaning Tower crashed down on the center of

the *Rhine Rose's* deck, shuddered, and remained there for a minute, connecting the two boats like a bent, sagging bridge.

The monkeys wasted no time. Screaming with fright, they flew like a cloud of dark brown fur across the bridge between the two ships, scrambled up the railings on the boat's side, and leaped onto those sitting in wheelchairs.

That was enough for the attendants. They panicked, bolted for the interior of the ship, and slammed the doors behind them.

The senior citizens were on their own!

CHAPTER 14

"THEY GOT THEM!"

Shocked at the sound of the violent explosions, the injured, but still-conscious Dantzler and the three teens whirled around and searched the river behind. Swirling black smoke roared up the side of the *Rhine Rose* into sky.

"Where are Hoffmann's boats?" Penny cried. "I don't see them!"

"Neither do I!" said David, searching frantically for their deadly pursuers.

David turned back to the job of steering them safely at high speed through the boat traffic on the Rhine. They sped by another tour boat, then past two long cargo ships. "There's a landing!" he cried suddenly.

The injured Dantzler sagged in the left-hand seat behind the shattered windshield, as Penny struggled to hold him upright. He opened his eyes at David's words, and looked to the shore. "That's it, David! Land there." Then he closed his eyes.

Behind them on the river, chaos reigned. The four

enraged hippos had reached the shore at a shallow spot, clambered up the inclining bank, crashed through a boat shed, and galloped away, as the walls collapsed behind them. The giraffes struggled to shore and clambered up the bank after the hippos. Hoffmann clung to the neck of one of the tall beasts as it began to gallop away. As the huge animal ran through a clump of bushes and picked up speed, Hoffman lost his grip and fell to the ground.

The frightened monkeys fared better. To the shocked surprise of the attendants aboard the Tranquillity Tours boat, the senior citizens had rallied to the aid of the terrified little animals, holding and comforting them, seemingly untroubled by their own sodden clothes and the shocks they'd endured. In fact, the group of passengers seemed delighted to be able to comfort the whimpering, drenched monkeys!

As the two boats picked up speed, the now bent Tower of Pisa fell into the water and slowly sank. Aboard the *Rhine Rose* a violent argument was taking place between the captain and the animals' foreman, who was raging at the loss of his precious animals.

Drawn by the smoke of the crashed motorboats and because of the frantic radio calls from other ships on the river, a police helicopter raced to the scene. It hovered over the river, propellers beating away waves in concentric circles. An officer shouted from a loud speaker, commanding the swimming skinheads and Fritz's henchmen to tread water where they were and wait for a police boat to pick them up.

A short time later, the phone rang in the office where Herr Kuli and Jim Daring waited anxiously for news of Mark, David, and Penny.

Kuli grabbed the instrument at once: "Ja?" he asked. He listened a moment, nodded, smiled, and then laughed out loud. "Gut! Gut! Danke!" Hanging up, he turned to Jim Daring. "That was Dantzler! He's bringing the kids here. He's injured, but not severely. His lifejacket saved him from being badly hurt by an arrow! He said they've had quite an adventure and he'll tell us all about it when he arrives."

"Thank the Lord!" Jim Daring said, vastly relieved. He'd been praying earnestly for their safety.

The phone rang again. Kuli picked it up. "Ja?" He listened . . . and listened . . . and listened. . . . Daring wondered what *this* call was about.

"Wunderbar!" Kuli exclaimed finally, and hung up. He turned toward Daring with a huge smile. "They got them, Jim! They got those men who came to pick up Dantzler's money! Paris, Bern, Frankfurt—they got them all!"

"Will Dantzler be hurt by this?" Daring asked anxiously.

"On the contrary, he's a hero! He's the reason the police got that network of Soviet and STASI agents! It's a great haul of spies. The police captain told me he's a hero twice over!"

"What a day!" Daring said wonderingly. "I can't

take it all in!"

"Neither can I, Jim," Kuli agreed. "Neither can I!"

Neither could Hoffmann. Drenched and cold from the river, his face bruised and bloodied, he'd dropped off the galloping giraffe as the beast crashed through a clump of bushes in its race to the park ahead. Since then, Hoffmann had crawled from bush to bush, ducking whenever he'd heard voices, determined not to be seen and reported to the police.

Fritz and the others must have been captured by the police, he reasoned. Then he thought of those American teenagers and cursed. Week after week this horrible summer, they'd continued to ruin his life! Utterly defeated, he crawled on through the bushes of the park. He *had* to get away unseen!

Late that afternoon, Penny, Mark, and David lounged with Daring, Kuli, and Dantzler in Kuli's office. Dantzler's shoulder was now covered by a bulky white bandage and he was pale, but he was OK. They had shared the adventures of their day, and astounded Jim Daring and Herr Kuli at the dangers they'd gone through.

Daring turned to Dantzler. "It was marvelous the way you got these kids out of danger!" he said admiringly.

"They saved my life, Jim," Dantzler replied. "That *Crossbowman* had me in his sights until David yelled and warned me to drop to the ground. Then he maneuvered the boat to drive both of Hoffmann's boats into that ship! And finally, they got me safely to shore. I'd say the four of us make a great team!" He beamed at the three teenagers. Penny hugged his good shoulder.

"And all the men who tried to get the money in those different cities were captured by the police?" she asked.

"They were indeed, Penny!" Kuli answered. "Thanks to that diskette of Herr Dantzler's, we were able to get the information to the police. They called their contacts in all the cities, and arrested all of the men as they came to the banks for the money."

"And they're in jail now, under heavy security," Dantzler said gratefully.

"That's great!" Jim Daring said. "Henri told me on the phone that this was a splendid haul of Soviet and Soviet-directed espionage agents!"

"Did they catch Hoffmann, Dad?" Mark asked eagerly.

Jim Daring frowned. "No, Mark, they didn't. Somehow he got away."

"Again!" Penny exclaimed. "Daddy, won't we *ever* be rid of that man?" She had a dreadful suspicion that they would encounter him again—somewhere, sometime.

"Sure we will, honey!" Daring told her. "Remember, all the others have been captured." "Their plot's been wrecked! Incidentally, Henri asked me to say hello to you three and to warn you to stay out of trouble!"

"Now he tells us!" Mark exclaimed, and they all laughed. "Boy, we could have used him today!"

"Well, as Shakespeare said," his father observed, " 'All's well that ends well!' We thank the Lord that you all came back safely."

Kuli laughed suddenly. "They've finally rounded up those hippos and giraffes that went into the river! They had a terrible time getting them back on the boat! The hippos smashed several boat sheds to splinters when they came out of the water. Then they ploughed through an open market, scattering people and tables of produce on their way! What a scene that must have been!"

"But you say they got them all back?" Daring asked.

"Yes, they finally did."

The three teenagers looked over at Dantzler. He, too, was remembering the wild chase on the river. Suddenly he smiled. "What a cruise!"

CHAPTER 15

TO THE GLORY OF GOD!

Early in the afternoon of the following day, Penny and her father sat at a table outside a fashionable restaurant on the Königsallee, watching the passersby and waiting for the boys to return.

"Daddy, that's wonderful of Mark and David to meet Karl and Willi in their church and lead them in prayer for commitment to God!"

"It is, indeed, Penny," her father agreed, smiling. "They've given those German boys hope. The four of them are going to read about the German Christian knights in the Middle Ages who dedicated their lives to defending Christian pilgrims on their way to the Holy Land. Those knights trained themselves to love God, to honor women, and to fight to protect the weak from violence. Then the four boys are going to pray in the church and ask the Lord's help to make them men of faith, purity, strength, and purpose. They too want to be men who will also serve God and honor and protect women." Daring paused. "That's not all. They're not

117

just going to *say* those words; they're also going to write down the plans they each have to reach their goals. They want to be the right kind of husbands and fathers when the time comes for them to take on those responsibilities. They know that they have to train themselves now if they want to become strong, upright men of faith."

Jim Daring looked soberly at his lovely daughter sitting there dressed in a flower-print jumper and long-sleeved white blouse. He went on, "Their motto is, 'To the Glory of God!' That's what they want to live for. That's what they want to be willing to die for." He was silent for a moment as he looked into her eyes. Then he smiled. "I'm so proud of them and I'm proud of you!"

"But Daddy, Mark and David are already the kind of men you describe!" she said, putting her hand on her father's arm. "You and Mom, and David's folks, too, have raised them that way."

"You've been a big part of it, Penny," her father said seriously. "Women and girls have to encourage men to be the right kind of men, or most of them won't rise to the challenge. You've been the kind of girl boys want to honor and protect. It takes teamwork to raise boys properly; you've helped in more ways than you can ever know."

Penny didn't know what to say. Her father had said this to her before. She knew he meant it, but at her age she couldn't yet realize how true it was. One day she would.

"Don't eat all that chocolate pastry!" Mark's voice broke into their thoughts. "We're starving!" He stood behind Penny and stroked his sister's head affectionately.

Penny laughed. The solemn mood was broken, but she knew she wouldn't forget her father's words. She smiled at Mark as he pulled out the chair beside her and sat down. David sat across the table. "Hi!" he said to her. She smiled back.

"Why would spiritual boys like you need mere ordinary food?" She teased. "Don't you set your mind on higher things?"

"Not when it's time to set my mind on food!" Mark replied. "This Christian life is complex, Penny. I keep telling you that! We need to be spiritual and all that, *and* we need to eat! If we don't eat, how can we be spiritual?" Mark looked over at his friend. "Order some of that German chocolate, David, while we've still got the strength to eat it."

Jim Daring and Penny laughed as David waved the waiter over. After David had ordered for himself and for Mark, Mr. Daring asked about Karl and Willi. "How are the German boys?"

"Dad," Mark replied, his face breaking into a huge smile, "they're great! Their mom has really kept them together these past years. And they've got a whole new vision of what they can do, and the kind of guys they can become."

"I don't think this is just an emotional kick, either,

Uncle Jim," David added. "They're really serious. Herr Kuli's friend, Herr Conrad, takes his son to karate school. He's agreed to let Karl and Willi work in his store, so they can earn money for their karate training. He's also gotten them into a Bible study with his church."

"They had never heard about the Bible studies, before" Mark added.

"That's great!" Jim Daring said approvingly. "You know, everybody in the American churches thinks that teenagers need to be with other teenagers. While teenagers do need friends their own age, they also need more time with adults. They need time with their parents, *and* they need time with other older friends. And boys have got to have time with men!"

"We told them about your invitation, Dad," Mark added. "They said they and their mom would love to join us all for dinner tomorrow."

The waiter came then with the chocolate pastries.

"Oh, Daddy, I hate to see these fine boys so addicted to sweets!" Penny said, with a twinkle in her eye.

"We're *not* addicted, Penny! We just like sweets, I tell you!" Mark insisted.

"That's right," David agreed. "We could quit whenever we want."

"When's that going to be?" Penny asked, laughing.

"Not this week!" her father replied. "We're staying in Germany longer than I had thought. I need to take you three to Frankfurt the day after tomorrow."

"Frankfurt!" the three exclaimed, astonished and excited at the same time.

"But, Daddy, I thought we were going to go back to Paris from here!" Penny exclaimed.

"That was the original plan. But there's been a change. Some very interesting developments have arisen suddenly and I could use your help in Germany for a few more days. Unless, of course, you're bored, and want to go back to Paris." He leaned back.

"Not at all, Dad!" Mark said excitedly. "What can we do for you in Frankfurt?" He was leaning forward eagerly.

David and Penny were excited, too, and could hardly wait to hear the new assignment Jim Daring had for them.

"Well, let's hope this *next* job will be completely safe!" Daring said. "All the danger's past, now that those Nazis are captured, and this assignment has nothing to attract those thieves. So, you'll have a safe, probably boring, time for several days in Frankfurt. Boring, that is, compared with what you three have been doing these past three weeks!"

"Then if we're leaving Düsseldorf so soon, I've got to hurry to get the pictures I want!" Penny exclaimed.

"Want to take some now?" David asked. "Would you excuse us, sir?" he asked her father.

"Certainly, David, by all means! Just take care of her."

"Yes, sir!" David replied, grinning. Penny picked up her sweater and camera, and the two walked down the beautiful Königsallee with its stretch of river in the midst of the city. David took her hand as they crossed the street.

"Dad, have they caught Hoffmann yet?" Mark asked.

Jim Daring frowned. "Not yet, Mark. But Herr Kuli tells me that they think they will very soon."

"Hoffman always seems to get away, doesn't he," Mark said thoughtfully.

"Yes, but thanks to you three, he always gets away empty-handed!" Jim Daring replied. "I'll be glad to hear that he's behind bars." He rose from the table. "I'm going back to Kuli's office. Why not follow David and Penny—at a distance, of course—and keep an eye out for skinheads. I think those guys are underground at the moment, but you never know."

"Yes, sir," Mark said.

Jim Daring glanced at David and Penny across the street. "Give them a little time to themselves," he added with a grin.

"Right!" Mark grinned back. He rose and wandered after David and his sister.

A few moments later he saw Penny turn and look for him. She waved. He waved back, but kept his distance.

"David," she said thoughtfully as they walked hand in hand along the elegant promenade, "you boys and Dad are always watching out for me, to keep me safe aren't you?"

He smiled at the charming girl. "You bet we are!"

She smiled back happily, "Thanks!"

They began to talk about Frankfurt. What a pleasant, peaceful time they'd have there!

Awesome Adventures With the Daring Family

Everywhere Mark and Penny Daring and their friend David go, there's sure to be lots of action, mystery and suspense! They often find themselves in the most unpredictable, hair-raising situations. Join them on each of their faith-building voyages in the *Daring Adventure* series as they learn to rely on each other and, most importantly, God!

Ambushed in Africa

An attempted kidnapping! A daring rescue! A breathtaking chase through crocodile-infested waters! Can the trio outwit the criminals before the top secret African diamond mine surveys are stolen?

Trapped in Pharaoh's Tomb

The kids are trapped in an ancient Egyptian tomb. How will they escape before the air runs out? Will they be able to outsmart their rival?

Stalked in the Catacombs

Penny, Mark and David explore Paris . . . but their adversary is lurking in the shadows. Will they be able to outrun him through the dark catacombs beneath the streets of the city?

Surrounded by the Crossfire

Rival drug smugglers will stop at nothing to get what they want. Why are KGB agents following Penny? Will the kids get caught in the middle of the danger?

Chased at Sea

The trio is involved in an incredible hunt involving a catamaran, a Russian sub, helicopters and more! Will they find the courage and creativity they need to escape from their predicament?

Available at your favorite local Christian bookstore.

Breakaway
With colorful graphics, hot topics and humor, this magazine for teen guys helps them keep their faith on course and gives the latest info on sports, music, celebrities . . . even girls. Best of all, this publication shows teens how they can put their Christian faith into practice and resist peer pressure.

All magazines are published monthly except where otherwise noted. For more information regarding these and other resources, please call Focus on the Family at (719) 531-5181, or write to us at Focus on the Family, Colorado Springs, CO 80995.